PENGUIN BOOKS

DIARY OF A RICH KID: LOST IN SPACE

Malcolm Mejin is the author of the *Diary of a Rich Kid* series. He first started writing the series in 2017 for fun, never intending to publish it. However, with his friend's advice, he decided to self-publish the series, which spawned three books originally. *Lost in Space* is the first book in the series published under Penguin Random House SEA. His first attempt at writing began at six years old, when he tried to write a short fantasy story and turn it into a home-made book. Ever since then, he has never stopped writing. Malcolm Mejin is also a frequent fixture at both public and international schools during his school tour, which he uses as a platform to empower and inspire youths, and share his passion in writing.

OTHER BOOKS IN THIS SERIES

Diary of a Rich Kid: The Ghost of Mount Hantu,
Penguin Random House SEA, 2023

Diary of a Rich Kid:
Lost in Space

Malcolm Mejin

PENGUIN BOOKS

An imprint of Penguin Random House

PENGUIN BOOKS

USA | Canada | UK | Ireland | Australia
New Zealand | India | South Africa | China | Southeast Asia

Penguin Books is part of the Penguin Random House group of companies
whose addresses can be found at global.penguinrandomhouse.com

Published by Penguin Random House SEA Pvt. Ltd
9, Changi South Street 3, Level 08-01,
Singapore 486361

First published in Penguin Books by Penguin Random House SEA 2023

Copyright © Malcolm Mejin 2023

ISBN 9789815058956

Typeset in CoopForged by MAP Systems, Bangalore, India

www.penguin.sg

'Sigh . . . What can I do to make your day?'

Charlie said those words for the hundredth time, kneeling on the floor in front of me. His eyes were ready to burst into tears any second.

'There's nothing you can do. Just so you know, you're done for,' I said matter-of-factly, sipping the almost non-existent mocktail from my margarita glass. I could have asked my butler, Cat (yes, his name is Cat), to bring me another drink, but Charlie's theatrics were keeping me occupied.

'I feel really horrible, I do,' Charlie said, letting out a heavy sigh. Standing on his two feet now, he moped around the swimming pool deck as if he had just lost his best friend.

I sighed, plonking my glass on the small white side table as I slid off my chaise lounge. His antics were starting to get on my nerves.

Charlie was riddled with guilt for stealing my designer clothes recently. When I had caught him stealing, I was furious and flabbergasted that my so-called best friend would do such a thing.

He could have just asked. I would even lend him my mansion if he asked. It is no secret that my mansion has become his favourite hideout, where he always has a good time splashing about in the stunning outdoor guitar-shaped swimming pool. The sprawling green lawns surrounded by the well-manicured gardens in the background made the entire landscape even more enticing.

So how did Charlie end up stealing my clothes?

His stepdad, Alibaba, who owns more designer underwear than a Calvin Klein model, had banned Charlie from splurging after he came home with a spending bill over his credit limit one day. Alibaba had had enough, so he confiscated Charlie's credit card.

Alibaba also went to the extreme and donated Charlie's entire wardrobe to charities, causing Charlie to spiral into unimaginable misery. Charlie had nothing left to wear, except hand-me-downs from our other friend, Ken Pok.

KEN, THANKS FOR YOUR CLOTHES. BUT DO WE HAVE TO LOOK LIKE A PAIR OF SIAMESE TWINS?

Initially, Manda, Charlie's Botox-loving mom who has a pear-shaped face and an hourglass figure, went out on a limb, disapproving Alibaba's draconian measures. But Manda, being Manda—who thinks that Alibaba is always right—eventually sided with Alibaba.

So, of course, miserable old Charlie had to crawl to his best friend for some mental and emotional support, and eventually, sneaked out some of his buddy's clothes to preserve his sanity.

'Stealing is a crime, you know?' I said candidly, gazing into the shimmering clear pool water under the scorching sun. 'In some countries, you would have been stoned to—'

A terrified squeal came from a white-faced Charlie. 'Can you not be MORBID? I've apologized like a gazillion times already. I'm sorry for stealing. I was just in such a bad place.' Charlie flopped down on the chaise lounge next to mine, blowing a heavy sigh and rustling the few strands of hair on his forehead. 'Tell me what I can do to make it up to you. I don't want to lose our friendship because of this.'

I sighed again. I had sighed so much in the last fifteen minutes that I thought I might develop Sigh Syndrome. In a way, I really did feel bad for Charlie. Charlie was a nice soul, but he could be borderline annoying sometimes. Nevertheless, he was still my best friend, a brother I never had.

'Can you promise me that you WON'T ever steal again?' I said in a grave tone, sitting down by the pool as the water lapped against my toes.

Charlie plopped down next to me, his hand over his heart. 'I PROMISE! I feel so bad for stealing. It literally crushes my soul. I'm left with nothing but a strong conviction of guilt!'

Kuching's Drama King is officially back! He's so dramatic that it totally irks me sometimes.

Nothing on Charlie's face showed any sign of remorse except his guilt-stricken puppy eyes. How could I not forgive my best friend? I could see that he felt really (and I mean REALLY) bad about his itchy hands pilfering my clothes off the shelves, and my heart instantly softened.

'Okay,' I said magnanimously, a smile lifting my lips. 'That's settled then.'

Charlie let out a cheerful whoop, dancing around the pool manically. (It was a relief that he didn't strip stark-naked in the swimming pool with his celebratory mood on high now.) Shortly, he plopped down next to me again, a little out of breath from his chicken dance under the hot sun. His eyes widened like saucers.

'So how can I make you happy?' Charlie asked in a high-pitched voice, bordering on falsetto. 'Tell me what I can do to make it up to you, my bestest best friend in the whole wide world.'

I kicked my feet in the water, watching ripples circle my toes. My mouth curved into a tiny mischievous grin. To be honest, if Charlie was sincerely sorry for his actions, I'd be the happiest kid in the universe. He did look sincere; I'll give him that. Since he was insistent on being charitable, I might as well take up on the offer before it expired.

'Send me to the Moon,' I said slowly, watching Charlie's stupefied expression.

'Send you to the WHAT?!' Charlie repeated, tugging at a lock of his dyed-blondish hair. He blinked his eyes at me in a daze.

'I would like to go the Moon, if possible.' I've always been fascinated with the Moon since I was a toddler. I'd seen images of astronauts making their mark on the Moon, planting flags bearing their country and name. The feeling of being in such a remote place, so far away from the Earth, was terribly incredible and highly desirable.

Of course, I'd stated my intention as a joke, for I knew that going to the Moon was practically impossible. By a long shot. Even though my father, Patrick Jin, owns a massive wealth of giant corporations across the globe, I didn't, for a second, think that a feat such as going to the Moon, was possible. Dad didn't have any connections to the astronomical world, nor was he ever trained as an astronaut.

'BUT I CAN'T DO THAT!!!' Charlie cried disbelievingly, his expression turning doleful. 'I can't even buy my own clothes now, let alone send you to the Moon! Hello, I'm just a kid! Not your fairy godmother!'

A chuckle escaped my throat as I playfully splashed some water at Charlie, who retaliated by doing the same; we were like wet ducks now.

'Charlie, I know,' I said in a resigned tone. 'I was just joking. I really want to go to the Moon, but I know it's not possible. Not even my rich father can do that. Money can buy you good shoes, but not a spaceship.'

'Can your request be more practical?' Charlie huffed. 'Maybe something like buying you ice cream for the entire week?'

I licked the corner of my lips, practically salivating at the thought of yummy strawberry ice cream on a hot day like this. 'Done deal, Charlie. You read my mind.'

'Duh. That's what best friends are for.'

Just then, the sound of footsteps heading towards the swimming pool deck made Charlie and I to turn our heads around.

It was none other than my dad, the fabulous Patrick Jin, CEO of Jin Corporation Inc. He swooped in like a male model on a runway, clad in his designer checkered shirt paired with slim-fit black shorts; the sun caught his short, spiky hair, giving him the overall look of a model on the cover of a fashion magazine. There was seriously no one like him in this world.

'Kids,' Dad said calmly, sitting on the chaise lounge with the air of a model trying to pose. 'I overheard your conversation.'

'You WHAT?!!!' Charlie and I said in unison. A blush crept up to my cheeks. What if we said something silly and Dad secretly recorded it and posted it on social media? I would never live to see another day.

'About you wanting to go to the Moon.'

Dad's response couldn't be more cryptic about us—or myself to be exact—wanting to go to the Moon. What could Dad do? Build an artificial moon that dangled over our house?

'Dad, please do not take us to the planetarium,' I practically begged, sitting back on my chaise lounge and began sipping the non-existent mocktail from my margarita glass again.

The last time we went to the planetarium, Charlie fell asleep on the wide crater of a man-made Mercury replica after hours of listening to the tour guide rambling about constellations and whatnot. Ken Pok, our nerdy friend whose brain has the capacity of a national library, was obsessed with the tour, gawking at almost every exhibit. Sometimes, I do think that Ken comes from a different planet than us. But I totally adore him; he keeps me grounded with his logical sense and simplicity.

'Who said anything about the planetarium?' Dad said, eyeing me sceptically.

'Then what is it this time?' I asked, possible locations whirling around in my head like a wild tornado. 'An amusement park with a Moon theme? A Moon museum?' Okay, I wasn't entirely sure if an amusement park would devote itself to the Moon, but it was worth a try.

'Better than that. You're all going to the Moon! For real!'

My heart shot upwards to my throat. Ding dongs began ringing in my head. Did Dad just declare that we were going to the Moon?

The real Moon? The one where Neil Armstrong landed???

That's lit!

I was so happy that I couldn't help but squeal, bouncing around and linking arms with Charlie, performing a weird dance I didn't even know existed.

'We're going to the Moon!!!' Charlie and I screamed simultaneously, accompanied by our boisterous chicken dance. We almost fell into the pool. Who cared about falling into the pool anymore?

We were going to the Moon, and I could fall into the pool multiple times without a care in the world!

'How is this possible, Dad?!' I asked, panting, my body trembling with excitement, while Charlie cartwheeled across the pool deck with a few hoots before joining me again.

'I bought a spaceship from NASA just recently,' Dad said coolly, as if that was the most natural thing to do—buy a spaceship! 'They put it up for auction, and I was the highest bidder. So now, I own a spaceship. It is a spaceship meant for leisure travel. Since it is now mine, I'm going to refurbish the spaceship with amenities such as comfy beds, deluxe bathrooms, and things that will blow your mind!'

Charlie and I hugged Dad so tight that we practically choked him.

'How many will it fit?' Charlie asked, his eyes twinkling and his body shuddering with wild excitement.

Dad smiled his signature Jin smile, a lopsided curve of the lips. 'Enough for all your friends!'

My heart raced. That meant I could bring Ken along who was sure to go crazy. Ken knows all about stars and constellations, so this trip would mean the world to him. And if the girls—Siti, Chloe, and Devi—knew that they would receive the invitation to the wildest trip of their lifetimes—they would be in seventh heaven by now.

'There's only one thing to do now,' Dad enunciated each word with an air of mystery.

'What?' I asked.

'You all need to go for some spacesuit shopping!' Dad cried. 'I've specially flown all customized spacesuits to Kuching so we can fly up to space in style!'

My jaw dropped, and I sneaked a quick look at Charlie. Charlie's jaw dropped all the way to the floor that he had to pick it up. Okay, he was probably TOO STUNNED to comprehend our starry, starry fate.

'And it's all on me. Choose whatever spacesuits you love.'

Charlie collapsed onto the floor, to the brink of unconsciousness before opening his eyes. In a split second, he erupted into a fit of giggles as he flapped his imaginary snow angels on the floor.

'I'm the happiest kid alive' Charlie declared, rolling around on the floor in ecstasy before finally tumbling into the pool and splashing water on me.

'Do you know what makes me happy?' I said with a wide grin.

'Going to the Moon?' Charlie said, giggling non-stop.

I jumped into the pool, splashes of water rising around me. I resurfaced, a smile plastered on my face. 'Going to the Moon with you all. My friends. My family.'

It just couldn't get any better than that.

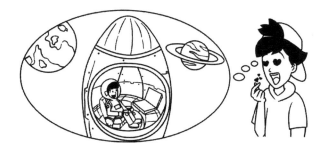

A MONTH LATER AT A SECRET LOCATION

Dad wasn't kidding when he said we would travel to space in style.

In a dimly lit hallway, which looked like the inside of a road tunnel, although on a smaller scale, Charlie pranced around in his polka-dot cream-colored spacesuit, looking like a fashion model on a runway.

'This is delightful,' Charlie said, a grin on his face as he sashayed up and down the length of the narrow hallway leading to the space launchpad. 'Can I kiss your dad, like, ten times? He has made space travel so chic.'

I stifled a giggle. To be honest. He looked like his whole body had popped out with pimple spots; Charlie looked like the Pimple Ambassador. I looked down at my spacesuit, which was plastered with a big yellow star, a smile breaking on my lips. I felt like a space superstar, just moments away from making a giant leap for mankind. Okay, Neil Armstrong had pretty much covered that. But still ...

CHARLIE, YOU LOOK LIKE MR PIMPLES.

My friends were all clad stylishly: Ken, wore a nondescript, patternless white spacesuit; Siti went all glittery pink; Chloe slayed with a checkered style; and Devi was all stripes.

And guess who else was going for the space trip?

Manda and Alibaba! Can you believe it? Charlie's mom and stepdad had to crash our space party. Dad allowed them to go on the trip because Alibaba made generous contributions to Dad's charity foundation.

I wondered what would it be like for them to be on this trip with us; Manda is known for showing public displays of affection with Alibaba—which can totally gross anyone out.

Mom, Dad, Manda, and Alibaba had chosen to wear the standard white spacesuit because they didn't want to stick out with patterned suits; simplicity can look quite chic too sometimes.

So Dad had whisked us off to a secret location, which was a private island just north of Sarawak, sealed off to the public as Dad had bought the whole island to build his space launchpad.

Can I scream out how COOL my father is?

The passageway to the launch pad was lit by a long row of wall light scones shaped like space shuttles, lit by a long row of wall light scones, shaped like space shuttles. At the end of the tunnel was a revolving glass door.

'I feel like we're going to heaven or something,' Charlie said.

'Charlie,' I huffed, screwing up my eyes in a pained expression. 'You're making it sound like we're going to die. Touch wood, touch wood.' Unfortunately, there was no wooden material in sight; the structures around us were either metal, brick, or plastic.

Charlie had to add insult to injury. 'Well, I see the light at the end of the tunnel.'

I groaned, irked by Charlie and his strange euphemism, but his obnoxiousness was soon dwarfed by Manda's first-world problems.

'I hope when we get to space, the anti-gravity doesn't wrinkle my skin,' Manda tutted, fingering her baby-smooth skin that was so firm that balls could bounce off it like off a ping pong table. Just a month ago, she had rhinoplasty to make her nose so slim that one could barely notice its existence; it looked like a tiny whipped cream stuck to the center of her face.

'I'm sure it won't wrinkle your beautiful skin,' Alibaba said reassuringly. 'But if it does, there's always Botox.' And then, the sight of the two lovebirds kissing each other, almost caused the pastrami sandwich I had eaten this morning to burst out of my throat.

Was PDA like this really necessary? It was totally cringe-worthy. I hoped that, once we finally reached space, the ever helpful anti-gravity would tear them apart and send them floating away from each other for good.

Eventually, we made it to the end of the tunnel and filed outside through the revolving door to the open-air space launchpad. The entire site was hidden from the outside world, concealed by a fifty-foot brickwall fence. Beyond the fence, I could see lush hints of the jungle.

My jaw dropped at the sight of a blue-colored space shuttle that towered like a giant ball-point pen, flanked by a winding staircase that led all the way to the top, where the entrance was.

'Blue???' Ken cried, his eyes twinkling.

'Of course,' Dad said with a smug smile on his face. 'White is so overrated. We need to add a splash of color to our space shuttle, you know.'

'You should have the shuttle painted pink,' Siti said with a giggle. Pink is her favorite color, and Siti always tries to wear something pink every day, if she can help it.

'Maybe in the future. The success of our leisure space travel will pave the way for more colorful space shuttles!'

My heart pounded in my chest as we ascended the stairs. I couldn't peel my eyes off the majestic space shuttle, which, in fact, kind of looked like a giant blue banana, and I felt like a teeny-tiny ant crawling up.

'It even matches the color of my blue checkered spacesuit,' Chloe remarked with a grin. 'Maybe this is all destiny.'

Sometimes, I think that Chloe and Charlie are twins who were separated at birth. Chloe can be as dramatic as Charlie sometimes, and it's only natural she would say something like that. I mean, it was only a coincidence, not some intergalactic alignment.

Once we reached the top, I was almost out of breath, feeling like I had climbed to the peak of Mount Everest, and knowing that I was minutes away from traveling to space gave me a surge of adrenaline.

A middle-aged burly man, clad in a white spacesuit, greeted us at the arched entrance of the shuttle. Who was he, and what was he doing here?

'Hi, I'm Spacey,' he introduced himself, a smile plastered on his face as he shook our hands. 'I'm a member of the space crew, who will ensure that your space trip runs smoothly.'

'Spacey?' What an apt choice for a name.

'He works for me,' Dad said, putting an arm around Spacey. 'He's very dedicated to this leisure space travel program. We're going to be in excellent hands.'

'What happens if there's a space shuttle crash?' Charlie asked. 'Will be we covered by insurance?'

'Charlie!' I swatted him on the shoulder. Why must he always focus on deeply unpleasant things?

Dad butted in with a chuckle. 'Don't worry, Charlie. Did I mention that we were in "excellent" hands? Nothing bad is going to happen.'

Charlie didn't look entirely convinced.

'Come, let's step inside,' Spacey chirped, ushering us through the entryway and into a brightly lit foyer, which had a paneled floor made entirely out of glass, and embedded with neon lights.

It looked somewhat like a discotheque—minus the bright neon disco ball, of course.

'Welcome to Shuttle Robin!' Spacey announced, his lips curving into a wide grin.

A collective gasp echoed through the room as my friends swiveled their heads at me, their faces replete with shock.

'You have a space shuttle named after you?' Charlie said incredulously. 'How come you have everything named after you? Even your underwear?'

Okay, I didn't have underwear named after me. My cheeks felt hot as the realization that we were going to fly in a shuttle named after me dawned upon me like a dropped curtain veil.

'I hope you love the surprise,' Dad chirped, putting his arm around me. 'It's an early birthday gift for you. You've always told me that you love space. So I think this is the perfect gift for you.'

Charlie groaned, his face as green as the cabbage in my backyard, and he turned to look at Alibaba with sad puppy eyes. 'Stepdaddy dearest. Can I have a space shuttle for my birthday?'

Besides Dad, Alibaba is also one of the wealthiest men in the world, his businesses mostly dealing with oil in Saudi Arabia; occasionally, he pampers Charlie with lavish gifts, but he tries not to go overboard.

'Sure,' Alibaba said with a cheeky grin. 'I'll buy you a space shuttle toy.'

Charlie gasped in horror. 'That was not what I had in mind.' But he knew he was defeated. There was no way Alibaba would ever buy him a real space shuttle. Alibaba may be extravagant at times, but he is mostly grounded—except when it comes to Manda, I think.

Charlie's predicament was soon forgotten when Spacey pressed a button on the wall, causing the floor to vibrate and slide away partially to reveal a winding staircase descending to another chamber. We scrambled down the staircase into a peculiar room, which had floor-to-ceiling glass windows facing the outside. Upholstered long benches sat by the windows on either side of the room.

'This is the observation deck, where you can view the space close-up,' Spacey explained, plopping down on one of the benches and motioning for everyone to follow suit. With a wink, he added, 'Who knows you may catch a passing asteroid? Shall we all buckle up now for take-off soon?'

'How about a tour of the rest of the shuttle?' I asked, hoping that there would be something dope inside the space shuttle, like a game room or even a cinema.

'We have time for that later. But now, let's prep ourselves for the launch.' Spacey whipped out a black rectangular remote and swiftly pressed a few buttons, activating the automatic seatbelts, which fastened around our waists. He then communicated some instructions, through his walkie-talkie, to the site crew in preparation for take-off.

My heart drummed against my rib cage as a frisson of excitement swelled within me. I couldn't believe that, in a minute or so, my family, friends, and I were going to shoot up into the stars.

'Are you guys ready for the launch of a lifetime?' Dad asked with a cheerful whoop, both arms raised. Everyone starting whooping and cheering.

Spacey finally said the magic words: 'Ready to launch.'

I gripped the edge of my seat tightly, my mind spinning in a momentum that could defy the law of physics, as shudders of excitement raced through my body.

Shortly after, a computerized voice boomed over the PA speaker, counting down. 'We're ready to launch in ten, nine, eight, seven, six, five, four, three, two … ONE!'

A thundering boom, almost like an atomic bomb, erupted causing tiny tremors rippling all over us, and suddenly, I felt my whole body shoot upwards rapidly as the space shuttle finally took off, making my insides to churn.

We were heading to space!

CAN I GET A HALLELUJAH???!!!

Charlie retched, his face completely ashen, looking like he was about to vomit out the chocolate bars he had eaten right before boarding the space shuttle.

'Charlie, are you okay?!' I asked, my eyebrows twitching.

'I think I'm going to be sick!' he croaked, clutching his stomach, his face as pale as Mandy's thick foundation-layered face.

But the dramatic sight outside the window tore my gaze away from Charlie for a second, and I couldn't help but marvel at the clear skies rushing in a cinematic blur, the sunny blues dimming into gradual darkness as we entered space.

'Are we in space already?!' Siti cried, slumping forward.

The thundering boom the thundering boom of the launch was now replaced by mere silence and a strange stillness that settled over everyone as we gazed at the dark void peppered with faraway dots of light, which I reckoned were stars.

Tiny gasps of awe reverberated through the chamber as everyone gawked at the dark, mysterious world that had intrigued mankind for generations.

A sense of weightlessness washed over me, and there was a dizzying throb in my temples.

'It's normal to feel a little dizzy or weak in space,' Spacey said, unbuckling his seatbelt and floating around the chamber above us, much to our awe. 'Don't worry. You'll all adapt to it after a day or two.' He then pressed a few buttons on his handheld remote and our seatbelts unbuckled. Soon, our bodies slowly floated up from our seats and we drifted haphazardly across the chamber.

'Look! We're flying!' Chloe cried brightly, her hands flailing about like a helpless chicken suspended in mid-air. 'Oh my God! I've never felt so happy in my entire life!'

Siti spun around like a yarn ball, giggling from the excitement and taking selfies on her mobile phone. 'Weeeeeeeeeeeee!' she squealed, occasionally bumping into another person in her way.

Charlie was unusually quiet, shrinking away to the corner and putting his hands over his mouth.

'Charlie, are you okay?' I asked, enjoying the sense of weightlessness as I drifted around, my body in a horizontal position and my arms wholly outstretched.

'I-I think I have an upset stomach,' Charlie stuttered, retching again.

'There's a plastic bag in the corner in case you feel like throwing up,' Spacey said, gesturing at the plastic bag dispenser.

Before Charlie could reach for the plastic bag, he did the unthinkable—his throat finally gave way in an awful retching noise. Gooey muddy chocolate burst out from his mouth, floating around the chamber like animal poop hanging in the air.

'Charlie, that's gross!' Devi cried in horror, dodging the chocolate vomit headed her way.

Instead of enjoying the extraterrestrial view outside, we got busy dodging Charlie's chocolate vomit that floated randomly in every direction before landing with a splat on Manda's horrified face.

'Ahhhhhhhhhhhh!' Manda screamed, brushing off the vomit from her face like it was some kind of a sticky disease. 'My face has been contaminated!!!'

Alibaba floated over to Manda, wiped the gooey thing off her face, and wrapped an arm around her in an obvious attempt to console her wretched soul. 'Manda, it's alright, darling. Hush, hush now. A kiss will make you feel better.' And with that, Manda received a sloppy kiss from Alibaba's puckering lips.

Okay ... it was my turn to vomit now. Did they seriously have to PDA like this? I was mentally scarred for life.

Apparently, Alibaba's kiss of life saved Manda's 'life-threatening' predicament. Manda was all smiles now, as if the vomit had never touched her face at all.

Alibaba's kiss certainly had its uses here in space, especially when it concerned Manda's 'emergencies'.

'I feel much better now after vomiting,' Charlie said calmly, his face flooded with relief. 'It's like my soul has been purged of evil.'

I rolled my eyes. Charlie made it sound as though he had been possessed by demons, when it had all along been the poor chocolates making the journey down Charlie's esophagus—alas, they didn't quite make it.

With Charlie's vomit still running amok we kept dodging trying our very best to contain his puke with the plastic bags that Spacey had graciously handed to us.

This wasn't how I had imagined our space voyage to be like—bagging Charlie's vomit.

After a quarter of a half-hour had passed, we were successful in completely capturing Charlie's barf in plastic bags. Then we disposed them off in the nearby litter bin.

We resumed our activities, gazing into the inky expanse of space while floating around in total abandon.

'My skin feels completely smooth,' Manda remarked, fingering her cheeks, her eyes twinkling with a lively spark. 'I think it must be the low gravity. If only I could live in space forever. No more wrinkles. No more gravity to tug at your skin, creating jowls and hideous whatnot.'

I stifled a giggle, amused at Manda's obsession with looking as young as a three-year-old baby; her relentless pursuit of youth was comical, albeit a tad annoying.

'I'll build an anti-gravity capsule for you down on Earth, my love,' Alibaba cooed.

Manda's eyes widened. 'You'd do that for me, darling?'

'Of course, I'd move the ocean, earth, and ... space for you.'

Okay, cue my vomit. This mushiness was making me sick.

Ken then pulled out his cellphone, held it close to his lips, and started to do a voice recording, detailing his journey from the moment of launch to being in space; his lips moved up and down hastily as though he were a mad scientist recording monumental observations.

Only N-E-R-D-Y Ken would do something like that. Couldn't he just loosen up a little? Well ... come to think of it ... I actually couldn't care less if he started taking biopsies from space organisms ... as long as he wasn't cramping my style.

'How do you like your advanced birthday gift, Robin?' Dad asked, wrapping an arm around me, floating side by side with me as we gazed into space.

'I couldn't have asked for a better gift,' I said, choking up with emotion because it was not a gift you can buy straight from the 'pasar malam', aka night bazaar, or a designer store--or any store on Earth, for that matter.

I would never take this gift for granted, ever. This was a gift that had touched the core of my soul, to the point that I almost felt like a changed human being, completely renewed.

Mom sidled up next to me, her black hair swirling about her face like the hair of a shampoo model in a TV ad.

'Your father and I have had discussed possible gifts during the early stages,' Mom revealed. 'We finally zeroed in on this when there was a space shuttle for auction by NASA. It was like BAM! GREATEST GIFT EVER FOR OUR SON!'

Mom owned a fashion company called Genetics, which has outlets in the entire world the entire world. Both Mom and Dad are highly successful entrepeneurs in their own right, but I could have never imagined that they would think out of the box and choose this out-of-this-world birthday present for me!

'Robin, can I be your half-sibling?' Devi implored dryly, floating right next to me. 'I hope your parents can adopt me.'

I chuckled with a shrug. 'I don't know . . . but I kind of like to be the only child.'

Devi screwed up her eyes in mock annoyance. 'Fine. Let me know when there's an opening, okay? I want to be the first to sign up.'

Spacey clapped his hands for attention, his body upside down now, a bemused look on his chubby face.

'Everyone, I think you guys are enjoying the sense of weightlessness, right?' he said slowly, hovering about with his feet touching the ceiling. 'Let me show you what this space shuttle really has to offer.'

We huddled around Spacey, raucous whoops erupting.

My mind raced as anticipation surged through me. Would there be an indoor anti-gravity swimming pool? And if there was, how would it work? Would the water float in the air like masses of bubbles?

Spacey thrust his way toward a closed metal hatch below him, which I presumed would lead to other chambers within the shuttle.

'Everyone, be in for a treat of a lifetime!' Spacey chirped, grunting as he turned the hatch clockwise.

As he was about to lift the hatch open, all of a sudden, the whole space shuttle jarred violently, tossing everyone around as though we were items in a washing machine. We collided into one another painfully, as a deafening rumble sliced the air.

'AHHHHHHHHHHHHHHHHIIIIIIIII'

Screams broke out in tandem, chaos breaking out with no rhyme or reason, and pain shot through me as the entire space shuttle spun around uncontrollably, jerking me around like a useless toy.

WHAT WAS HAPPENING????????

WHY WAS THE WHOLE SPACE SHUTTLE SPINNING LIKE A YARN BALL UNRAVELING OUT OF CONTROL?

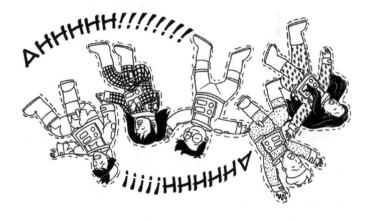

I screamed my lungs out, my heart drumming so hard that my rib cage felt as though it was about to be torn apart.

Fear shot through my veins.

Were we going to die??????

The torturous spinning ensued for what seemed like a fifteen minutes. Our horrified screams crescendoed, almost rupturing my eardrums.

Charlie's backside whacked my nose—it was a good thing he didn't fart or I would have died.

We collided, hard and painfully, with one another, bumped into walls, and hit our heads against the ceiling.

Then all of a sudden, the dizzying movement came to a grinding halt; no tremors could be felt, and everything became stationary once more.

'WHAT JUST HAPPENED???' Dad snarled, his fiery eyes throwing a sharp accusatory look at Spacey as though he was solely responsible for the pandemonium.

Spacey's jaw dropped, his face slightly flushed. 'I-I don't know,' he stuttered, his hands going over to his mouth. 'I seriously don't know.'

'What do you mean you don't know???' Dad demanded furiously, crossing his arms over his chest. 'You are part of my space crew, who's supposed to make sure that the space shuttle is in top-notch condition! I paid billions for this space shuttle!!!'

Even Manda was infuriated, her eyes throwing dagger looks at poor old Spacey. 'My face could have been ruined by the endless tossing!' She fingered her under-eye areas, her eyes squinting in misery. 'I think I just grew a new batch of crow's feet!!!'

I rolled my eyes at Manda's irrationality. Was beauty her prime concern? We could have died, for crying out loud!

Before Dad could explode in a tirade, the overhead intercom buzzed, stopping everyone in their mid-air tracks.

'Hi, everyone, this is Captain Muroe,' he said in a grave tone, sounding like he had just attended a funeral. 'I'm the space shuttle pilot, responsible for steering this vessel. There was an equipment failure in the maneuvering thrust, causing the entire space shuttle to spin out of control. However, my technician team has expeditiously fixed the problem, and everything is back to normal again. I can't stress enough how sorry I am for the distress the incident may have caused all of you. It won't happen again, I assure you.'

Dad heaved a heavy sigh, the muscles in his jaws beginning to relax. The red shade on his face was slowly fading away. 'Let's hope this doesn't happen again. If it does, I'm going to sue all the operations team!'

'I thought we were going to die or something,' Devi said shakily once Captain Muroe had signed off, her face still a little blanched. 'I've never felt so scared in my entire life.' Tears began to stream down her cheeks.

I swiveled a glance out the window at this seemingly infinite stretch of darkness, which looked like a giant black fabric, and my pulse quickened, a feeling of unease sweeping over me. We were practically in the middle of nowhere, in space, in the total unknown where our fate seemed to hang in the balance. What if one of the pressurized cabins exploded? What if an asteroid came out of nowhere and headed our way? What if—

I stopped thinking those negative thoughts. If there was one thing I've learned, it's better to live in the present moment that worrying about the what-ifs.

'Everyone, let's just chill, okay?' Spacey said brightly with a weak smile. 'Let's not let what happened spoil our moods. Shall I give you a tour of the rest of the space shuttle?' Spacey was obviously trying to lighten up the bleak mood.

We brightened up a little, but there was clearly some lingering tension in everyone's eyes. From then onwards, nobody brought up the subject about the incident again, as if it were a thing of the past that everyone wanted to forget.

We followed Spacey through another hatch, and ended up in a silver chamber filled all over with floating balls of dual colors: red and blue. They were the size of a ping pong ball, and were swirling languidly around us like bubbles. Hanging on the wall, on one side of the room, were what appeared to be white rifle-shaped guns, with garish orange tips.

Was this the war room? Why were there … guns??? Were we going to face off with evil aliens from outer space?

'This is the game room,' Spacey explained, grabbing a few balls with one large fist and flicking them into the air so they would float around again.

'GAME ROOM????!!!!' we all shrieked, baffled looks plastered on our faces as we stared at the two-colored balls.

'Yes, in case you guys get bored, you can play Balloutch, a space ball game specially designed for all of you by our creative team!'

'Wow,' Ken said. 'I could use a game or two to flex my brain.'

'How do you play the game?' Siti asked.

Spacey grabbed a gun from one of the hooks and snapped the piston. 'There's no gravity in space, so the balls will just float around you. I'm holding a thrust gun, which delivers a quick thrust of air from its muzzle. Aim the gun at only the red balls and flick them towards your opponent. The objective of the game is hit your opponent with the red balls and be awarded one point for each ball. There are no points for blue balls.'

Spacey then motioned a finger at a CCTV camera perched on the ceiling. 'This advanced CCTV camera, which has facial recognition capabilities, can recognize your faces and motions, and detect if a red ball has hit your opponent. The computer will automatically generate the scores.'

I held my breath, a rush of exitement surging through me. Balloutch sounded more exciting than floating around all day doing nothing.

'One game will last for fifteen minutes,' Spacey added. 'Are you guys ready to try it out?'

'I'm on board!!!!' Ken practically squealed. He is the kind of guy who would go crazy over games, encyclopedias, and math quizzes.

Spacey handed us transparent face shields for protection and our own airguns, then moved behind a plexiglass block at the far corner to watch us play Balloutch. He pressed several keypads on the wall panel, initiating the game.

On the wall in front of us was a huge LED display which showed us the countdown numbers. A computerized voice said: 'Game will begin in ten, nine, eight, seven, six, five, four, three, TWO and ONE!!!!!!' A loud buzzer sounded, signaling the start of the game.

We began flicking balls at our opponents with our airguns.

'Remember to only aim at the red balls,' I reminded myself mentally as I floated purposefully around the room, trying to locate Charlie.

Charlie and I are frenemies; we can be best friends one day, and enemies the next (in good faith, I mean). We're naturally quite competitive towards each other, so naturally, I will hunt him down first instead of the others. And of course, the same went for Charlie—he was trying to get me too.

'You're going down, Robin!' Charlie practically cackled like an evil witch, aiming his airgun at me.

'The same goes for you, pal!' I countered.

Charlie was so intent on getting me that instead of aiming at the red balls, he accidentally aimed at the blue balls, which hit me on the chest and bounced off.

I grinned. 'Blue balls? No points off for you!'

Deftly aiming my airgun at one of the red balls, I managed to hit Charlie square on the face (or his face shield, for that matter).

One point for me!

'No fair!' Charlie snarled, brandishing his airgun wildly and blasting away, only to hit the blue balls, which deducted more points for him.

I had to admit it—it was kind of hard to aim at the red balls because both color-coded balls were constantly floating around us. For instance, when you were aiming at the red ball right in front of you, a couple of blue balls might suddenly graze past and block your aim.

That was what was so challenging about Balloutch: the balls were constantly moving around in mid-air and posing obstacles that required deftness and quick maneuver.

Because I was so intent on dueling with Charlie, I didn't realize that I was an easy target for Devi, who was constantly aiming at me and raking up points for herself.

I began to realize that I was at a disadvantage, and if I kept pursuing Charlie mindlessly, I would lose the game. I had to target others too.

'Charlie, we have to watch out for others too! Call it a truce?' I said dolefully.

'Fine,' Charlie relented and began to shift his focus on others.

Devi aimed her airgun at me again and blasted the red ball toward my face, but I managed to dodge it in the nick of time.

'Hey, I thought you were an easy target!' Devi cried.

I grinned. 'Not anymore.'

I began aiming at Devi, who tried to dodge the red balls that blasted towards us, but several of them hit her, much to Devi's horror.

Devi scrambled, trying to elude me.

All of a sudden, I felt balls thumping against my back, which made me jerk around to see the face of my attacker: it was none other than my own father, who had a wide grin on his face!

'Dad! No fair!' I cried incredulously. 'I'm your only son.' If that last statement 'actually' helped.

'Well ... it's the battle between father and son!' Dad laughed.

'Fine!' I said in mock grumpiness, but burst out laughing as though I were being tickled, as Dad blasted balls at me. 'Game on!'

It was a scene of pure madness. Balls ricoheted off bodies as everyone fell into a mad scramble to blast their opponents. Even with Dad hunting me down, I wasn't completely safe; occasionally, I was someone else's target.

I tried, at my very best, to dodge balls flying toward me from different directions, as though there were missile strikes on me.

Siti, who used to take gymnastic lessons when she was six, twirled and swirled with ease, dogdging the balls. Ken moved about as though he were a robot, his small-frame body completely stiff and his eyes screwed up in deep focus. Manda seemed to be more on the defensive side, mostly shielding her face with her airgun as though she was afraid her nose would crack.

The buzzer finally sounded, signaling the end of the game, much to our relief. Although the game was enjoyable, it was pretty intense.

Spacey floated out from his safe spot, his face plastered with a wide grin, an indication that he probably knew who the winner was.

'WHO WON???!!!' Everyone wanted to know.

'I think I won,' Charlie said haughtily, holding his airgun proudly as though it was his prized possession. 'I felt like I aimed at dozens of red balls and hit all my targets.'

There was no way Charlie could have won. I'd seen him spend more time dodging balls in horror than trying to shoot. Or perhaps he got lucky.

'The winner is . . . ' Spacey said, imitating a drumroll motion with his hands, '. . . Ken Pok!'

Confetti exploded from the ceiling, raining down on us in a splash of rainbow colors. Strains of upbeat, jazzy music wafted through the room.

Ken wore a big smile on his face, looking like he could conquer the world—or space.

How could one tiny bespectacled boy have so many talents crammed into one body? How was that fair? He was athletically and academically gifted—and now, he was the Balloutch champion?

Could I have his genes, please?

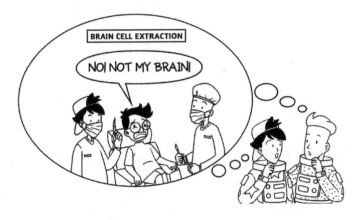

'I hate losing,' Charlie whined, his lower lip pouting so protrusively that he looked like a pufferfish. 'Can I drown my sorrows in ice cream? Wait. Can we eat ice cream in space? Is there any ice cream here?'

'Of course there is!' Spacey said brightly, floating squarely to the center of the room as though he were the sun orbited by the rest of us. 'There's a special NASA freezer which stores these multi-flavored ice creams.' That welcoming revelation was followed by a cacophony of happy whoops and clapping. 'But we have a limited supply of ice creams here. Since Ken is the winner, he gets to choose two astronaut ice creams of his choice!'

'Astronaut ice cream?' Charlie repeated, his eyes widening. 'Is that even a thing?'

'Who cares if it's a thing or not,' Siti said quickly, her drool practically floating out from the corner of her mouth. 'As long as there's ice cream, we will be A-okay!'

'We all scream for ice cream!!!' Dad cried boisterously, trying to achieve the air of a youth craving for ice cream.

I rolled my eyes. 'Dad, that's kind of corny. I've heard that phrase used, like, a gazillion times.'

'Follow me to the next chamber,' Spacey instructed, drifting toward another hatch behind Siti, who was taking endless selfies with her phone. Charlie floated beside Siti, twisted his fingers into a heart gesture, and smiled into Siti's camera phone.

'Photobomber,' Siti huffed, a wry smile plastered on her face.

No sooner had we started going through the hatch than a blood-curdling scream tore through the air. Our heads immediately jerked around to the source of the sound—Chloe.

'What's wrong, Chloe?' Mom asked, her brows furrowed with concern.

Chloe blanched, looking like she had seen a ghost, her frightful eyes staring out the nearest window beside her. We followed her gaze, trying to see what she was seeing.

'Wait, is there something outside?' Alibaba asked, frowning as he pulled Manda closer to his chest. Manda held on to him tightly as though he were her knight in shining armor.

We edged closer toward the window, screwing up our eyes to have a better look at the object lurking outside.

In the far distance, something fiery and luminous, seemed to be hurtling toward our space shuttle, a small dot of light zooming through space.

What was that thing? Could we even call it a thing? Or was it an alien from another dimension trying to raid our space shuttle? This rising paranoia within me was making me think irrational things.

Our heads crammed together near the window, we kept our eyes trained on the mysterious flying object.

'OH NO!!!' Spacey screamed, and I immediately saw the sheer horror gleaming in his eyes.

What had Spacey seen that had caused that fear?

Goosebumps prickled across my skin; I could feel his fear brushing off on me.

'What is it, Spacey?' I asked, my hands gripping Charlie's tightly, our bodies trembling in the suddenly chilly room. I could practically hear teeth chattering as everyone awaited Spacey's answer in the deepest of anticipation.

'It looks like a meteor!' Spacey screamed, his shaky hands clawing at his face relentlessly. 'It's going to hit us!'

IS THE METEOR REALLY GOING TO HIT US???

Spacey immediately spoke into his silver walkie-talkie, words trembling out of his mouth. 'CAPTAIN MUROE!!! DO YOU COPY??? SOMETHING THAT LOOKS LIKE A METEOR IS HEADING OUR WAY!!!'

The space shuttle pilot, Captain Muroe, replied almost instantly, his voice highly tense, a departure from his calm voice we had heard earlier on. 'I KNOW!!!! OUR SYSTEM HAS JUST DETECTED AN INCOMING FIERY UNIDENTIFIED OBJECT!!! WE'RE TRYING TO EVADE IT!!!'

'CAN WE EVADE IT IN TIME??? FROM WHERE I'M STANDING HERE, IT LOOKS LIKE IT'S RAGING FAST TOWARDS US!!!'

Our eyes swiveled from terrified-looking Spacey to the ball of light that grew brighter with each passing second, and ominously bigger too, if that helped.

'YES!!! WE'RE TRYING TO MANEUVER OUT OF ITS WAY!!!'

We were startled by the sudden, violent trembling of the entire space shuttle, which gave a thundering boom like a rumbling engine. I could feel the immediate tilt and acceleration of the space shuttle, which seemed like a last-ditch attempt to evade the incoming unidentified object.

'This is insane!!!' Dad cried, his terror-stricken eyes glued to the zooming fiery object. 'Just our luck! This had to happen today of all days when we're on our maiden space trip!!!'

'It's like the universe is conspiring against us,' Charlie added quickly, his teeth chattering as we all watched helplessly out the window.

'Charlie! Stop all this negativity!' I snapped, clutching his hand. 'We're going to be okay! Believe it, and it shall be true!' But the heavy thumping in my heart betrayed what I was really feeling.

We froze in terror as we watched the bright, orange strip of light, looking similar to a fire dragon, sailing towards us. Our horrified murmurs rippled through the room.

I was watching my life flash before my eyes as the flaming light approached.

Would we survive? Or would we die?

The meteor-like object was moving at lightning speed, slicing through the dark void ferociously, seemingly too fast for our space shuttle to dodge in time; from what I could roughly gauge, it would be less than a minute before it HIT US!!!!!!

'FASTER, CAPTAIN MUROE!!!' Dad yelled, the angry lines on his forehead deepening, his fists clenched to the point that they almost turned white. 'YOU'RE NOT MOVING OUT OF THE WAY FAST ENOUGH!!!!'

'WE'RE TRYING!!!!' Captain Muroe snapped back, his voice shaking. 'THE METEOR IS MOVING TOO FAST!!!'

Manda whimpered miserably, her hands shooting up to her face. 'Oh no, my face will be ruined by that crazy fiery thing!!!'

'Mom, we will be dead if we can't dodge it in time!' Charlie said shrilly, cowering in a far corner as if that would help him evade the disastrous object. 'There's no time worrying about beauty!'

The flaming object was too close for comfort.

I was sure that we would D-I-E. No miracle could save us now. Shuttle Robin was DOOMED!

As it loomed dangerously close, the light from the object became so glaringly bright that we had to shut our eyes our eyes against it, and our ears were greeted with the piercing sound of crackles associated with fires.

This was it. We were seconds away from death.

I jerked my eyes shut, clinging to whoever was the nearest to me as a cacophony of bloodcurdling screams filled the room. In a split second, the sound of a deafening explosion boomed, followed by a massive, violent tremor that rocked the entire space shuttle; we spun around fast and collided with everthing and everyone around us, pain slicing through my body.

'AHHHHHHHHHHHHHHHHIIIIIIIIIIIIII'

At the sharp, rising screams, my eardrums almost burst and my temples throbbed as though there were pounding drums inside.

Spinning haphazardly, I stole a quick peek at the sight of blurry bodies and the Balloutch floating balls spiraling around in a tornado spin. My insides churned so much that I felt extremely nauseous and sick to the core.

Before I knew it, everything suddenly came to a grinding halt.

The entire room stopped moving, as if someone had just slammed on the brakes, and the impact caused everyone to jerk to a stop, ending in a messy pile of bodies in the corner; everyone's limbs were splayed in awkward angles, and groans of pain filling the air.

Out of the corner of my eye, as I lay on top of Charlie, I saw Manda and Alibaba wrapping their arms tightly around each other as though they were a pair of Siamese twins.

Manda burst into tears, her mascara ruined. 'Is-is-is it over? Is it over?'

'I-I ... think so,' Alibaba replied slowly, his hand stroking Manda's back as if she were a stray cat in need of comfort.

Dad and Mom looked alright, except for the mild bruises on their faces.

I THINK MY NOSE JUST FELL I NEED PLASTIC SURGERY ONCE WE RETURN TO EARTH.

Spacey looked like a complete wreck, tears trickling down his ashen cheeks as he trembled uncontrollably. 'D-d-d-d-did we m-m-make it???'

'I think so,' Dad said stoically. He floated towards the window, peeked outside for a few moments, then swiveled his gaze to us. 'Okay, I think I know what happened. If Captain Muroe hadn't moved the space shuttle, that damned thing would have hit us squarely in the center and split everything into half, and we'd definitely have no chance of survival.'

'So that crazy fiery what-you-call-it hit our shuttle???' Charlie snapped, tense lines creasing his forehead.

'It did. From what I can see from this angle, it seems to have hit the rear end of our space shuttle, like a bullet graze. I'm afraid to think what would have happened if it hit right in the middle...'

Charlie's eyes bulged. 'Bullet graze????? The entire space shuttle shook violently‖‖ It felt like a bomb to me‖‖'

Before Dad could counter, the intercom buzzed, with Captain Muroe's voice on the line. 'Is everyone okay???'

'If you mean having bruises and permanent mental scarring okay,' Charlie said testily, crossing his arms over his chest. 'How could you do this to us???'

'I'm sorry. We didn't mean for this to happen... we don't even know what that "thing" is... it just came out of the blue, without warning. Because we tried to steer clear of the unidentified object, it hit the rear end of our space shuttle instead of the mid-section, where the vital system components are located. If it had hit those components, we could have...' There was a soft gulp on the line.

Everyone kept silent. We all knew what would have happened if the space shuttle was struck in the middle. OK, save the euphemism—we would have DIED.

Charlie wouldn't be able to wear his favorite Prada shoes anymore, nerdy Ken wouldn't be able to look at his germ collections through his microscope anymore, social media queen Siti wouldn't be able to take selfies anymore, Chloe wouldn't be able to do her favorite journaling anymore, and Devi wouldn't be able to look at cute boys wandering the earth anymore.

I wouldn't be able to eat my favorite Sarawak Laksa anymore.

ARE THERE SARAWAK LAKSAS IN HEAVEN?

'Luckily,' Captain Muroe continued, 'the space shuttle is functioning as per normal, so there shouldn't be a problem to continue our trip. Thank God none of us were seriously injured.'

'So where did that weird meteor-like thing go?' Dad asked as he looked out the window, his eyes cautiously darting back and forth as if the 'thing' would hit again. 'I hope it didn't hurtle its way towards . . . ' he said shakily with gulp, '. . . Earth.'

'No, no, no. It didn't,' Captain Muroe said reassuringly. 'We've checked our radar. That "thing" grazed past Earth, just inches away from the stratosphere, but never really breached its way into Earth. Our planet is safe.'

I CAN'T BELIEVE WE WERE ALMOST KILLED BY THAT 'THING'.

Dad's face turned purple, his nostrils flaring. 'Were our space scientists sleeping on the job??? How did they fail to predict this strange space phenomonon and alert everyone??? I forked out so much money for this space trip, and I can't believe our life was almost on the line just because our team didn't do their job well!'

'Can we put Jorge on the line, please?' Captain Muroe said immediately, his voice sounding edgy.

'Who's Jorge?' Mom asked.

'He's the head scientist who's supposed to look out for any dangers lurking in space and warn us,' Dad growled. 'It seems like I will have to FIRE HIM!!!'

'Hi, it's me, Jorge,' a sudden, brash voice came on the line. 'I'm the head scientist. I'm so sorry for what had happened ... but—'

'BUT WHAT???? There aren't supposed to be buts on this trip!!!! I shelled out billions of dollars to make this space trip a reality, and now you're giving me buts???'

'Take a chill pill, hubby dear,' Mom said, stroking Dad's shoulder. 'Let him explain.'

'She's right,' Manda agreed, her slim fingers scuttling across her face as if she were checking for flaws. 'You'll get more wrinkles and grow white hair if you get overly stressed.'

MOM, EVEN IF YOU GET WRINKLES, I'LL STILL LOVE YOU.

CHARLIE, I'M TOUCHED. BUT NO TO WRINKLES FOR ME.

I rolled my eyes. Only Manda could be constantly offering unsolicited beauty advice.

'This strange and unique phenomenon we have just witnessed is known as the ... ' Jorge continued ominously, 'darkensom meteor.'

'DARKENSOM METEOR?' all of us said simultaneously.

'The darkensom meteor is a new phenomenon, something recently discovered by scientists...'

'Wait a minute,' Ken interrupted, his eyebrow arched. 'I find this really strange and totally impossible! Meteors do not exist in space!'

Loud gasps rippled among everyone as we turned our gaze towards Ken, who looked like a nerdy astronaut about to spout some scientific theory.

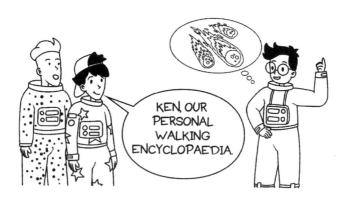

KEN, OUR PERSONAL WALKING ENCYCLOPAEDIA.

'What do you mean meteors do not exist in space?' Devi asked in a weary tone, her head slumped against Siti's shoulder.

'Meteors should not occur in space at all!' Ken explained, his eyes gleaming, 'Meteors come from asteroids. When these asteroids enter Earth's atmosphere, air compresses quickly, and they heat up and burn brightly. So factually, asteroids simply do not heat up in space without air friction!'

I got to give it to Ken for always being our reliable walking encyclopedia. Who needs Google Assistant or Siri when you have this bespectacled wonder with a small head but a big brain?

'So why do we have meteors running amok in space???!!!' Charlie cried incredulously, looking completely perplexed.

Jorge's somber voice returned to the intercom. 'That's what's so puzzling! Only a very few in the astronomical community know about this new phenomenon, which was recently discovered by a Canadian scientist named Alberta Wichs, who had captured the meteor via a space radar. But it wasn't publicized because Alberta wanted to do more research first. Based on her shocking findings, there's actually a small pocket of air floating around in space, which causes this friction with a passing asteroid. She termed this pocket of air as "airibum". Airibums are scattered across the length of space, invisible to the naked eye so we can't exactly pinpoint their location. Simply put, just think of airibums as small invisible balloons carrying air around space . . . and there could be millions of them floating around!'

'But I thought there's no air in space!' Chloe squeaked, her eyes widening with puzzlement.

'Well, that's not true anymore. The astronomical community is now trying to locate those scattered airibums, and hopefully we'll have equipment advanced enough to track them down.'

'Airi-what?' Charlie said, a trance-like look on his face.

'Airibum,' I enunciated, fear welling inside me. Space was indeed a mysterious world, vast and infinite ... but it could be scary as hell. God knew what sort of things were lurking out here ...

'Look, don't you guys worry about this,' Jorge said reassuringly, but the strain in his voice betrayed him. 'You should continue enjoying your space trip. My crew and I will do our utmost best to give advanced warning should such phenomenon occur again. Trust that you're all in good hands ... and enjoy your space travel!' Jorge finally signed off, followed by a still silence and a collective feeling of unease.

Dad sighed with a hint of a smile, his eyes roaming everywhere around him and his shoulders slightly relaxed. 'Look, from this moment on, let's just enjoy our trip, okay? We didn't travel all the way up to space just to stress ourselves up. What is past is past, and I pray that we won't have to face the ducky meteor—'

'Darkensom meteor,' Ken corrected quickly.

'Darkensom meteor. Thank you, Ken. Anyway, what I was trying to say is . . . let's live in the present moment. Enjoy the now instead of worrying about the future. Don't you all agree?'

There was a brief silence as everyone contemplated what Dad had just said. Charlie looked deeply puzzled, as though Dad had mentioned an extremely complicated philospical theory.

I couldn't agree more with Dad's statement, a tiny smile breaking across my lips. I truly believe that living in the present moment is the greatest gift we can give ourselves. Why add worry lines to our forehead when we can choose to be happy, right?

'I believe he's right,' Manda agreed. 'Don't dwell on the negative, but on the positive. That way, you'll always be in good spirits.'

'Ya,' Charlie said, a sarcastic edge to his voice. 'When you're in good spirits, fewer wrinkles will come to you, and then you don't need to waste money on Botox to save your skin from sagging like the rear end of a cow.'

Instantly, Manda gave Charlie a scowl, as if he were referring to her. Charlie, who realized his silly bluntness, reacted with a sheepish smile, hiding behind me in case Manda decided to claw his face.

When everyone had seemingly calmed down, Spacey clapped his hands for attention. 'I think we ought to call it a day and get some rest. Come, let me show you all to your sleeprooms.'

'Sleeprooms?' Charlie repeated, a confused look plastered on his face.

'In space, we call bedrooms sleeprooms. Call it space speak.'

Charlie heaved a sigh. 'I hope I don't have to learn more new space jargon. Like that ass-bums—'

'Airibums,' I corrected, rolling my eyes.

'Or words like dumby-som—'

'Darkensom,' I said curtly, shaking my head.

Charlie shrugged. 'How many weird words can you learn in a day?'

'They're not weird, Charlie. In fact, I find them quite fascinating.'

I wasn't usually fascinated with technical terms such as these, but being in space had totally changed my life; it was as though I had been given a new soul from the extraterrestrial world.

With Spacey leading the way through a maze of intertweaving chambers, we finally reached a silver-walled chamber filled with two bunk beds. 'One sleeproom won't be enough to fit everyone, so some of you will have to sleep in several adjoining sleeprooms.'

'Some of you kids can take this room,' Dad said decisively, floating toward the top of the bunk bed, his hands lightly touching the pillows. 'Won't the pillows float?'

'These pillows are designed with gravity enhancement so they won't float away,' Spacey explained. 'Each bed comes with a strap to prevent your bodies from floating away when you sleep.'

Charlie ran his hands down the length of the entire bed, his eyes gleaming. 'Wow, the softest pillow I've ever touched, yet firm, and the mattress feels as smooth as skin.'

'That's because these space bunk beds are made with expensive, high-grade material,' Spacey continued jauntily, a bright smile playing on his lips. 'Everything has been designed with quality and comfort in mind, making you feel like you're sleeping in a five-star hotel, and that's not all . . . '

He proceeded to press a yellow button on the wall beside him, and instantly, the metallic panels on each side of the walls slid away to reveal a floor-to-ceiling, clear-glass window, which offered a stunning full-angle view of space!

It was as though I was a small ant being dangled right in the middle of space, in this vast dark void that stretched infinitely. Floating fixed at the sight before me, I felt as though I was completely lost in time, in a world where there was no daylight to separate day and night.

I was in complete awe of this extraterrestrial wonder, but at the same time, had a nagging fear of the unknown.

'This is better than that luxurious 'sky' hotel I stayed in Paris last year,' Charlie reminisced, nuzzling the bunk bed pillow against his face. I sighed. Charlie had repeatedly told us about his unique stay at the hotel, where the room walls could turn transparent, offering a breathtaking, close-up view of the skies.

Seeing that Charlie, Ken and I had settled ourselves comfortably in the room, Dad said, 'The boys will take this room then.'

'How about us?' Siti asked, her long silky hair billowing around her shoulders.

'There are enough sleeprooms in this shuttle for everyone,' Spacey chirped. 'Robin's parents have their own private sleeproom, so will you girls, and Manda and Alibaba too.'

'Wow, this shuttle is bigger than I imagined,' I gushed, my thoughts drifting to the possibilities of other facilities built inside this space shuttle. Would there be an indoor swimming pool? A spa? God knew what other surprises awaited us next.

WILL THERE BE A
SPACE POOL?

'Where will you be sleeping then?' Chloe asked Spacey curiously.

'He's going to sleep in the space toilet,' Charlie said quickly.

Spacey chuckled at Charlie's dry humor. 'As part of the space crew, we have our own sleeping quarters, which are less ... um ... classy than the sleeprooms, which are reserved for special guests like all of you.'

Charlie yawned audibly, his lanky arms outstretched.

'Why don't all of you get some rest?' Dad suggested. 'When you wake up, there will be a special surprise for everyone!'

Everyone squealed excitedly at Dad's announcement. Whenever Dad has a surprise, it never disappoints.

So what could be the 'special surprise'? I wondered with a broad grin. As if the unique sleeproom providing the panoramic view of space itself wasn't enough. What could seriously top that?

'Will there be a swimming pool inside this space shuttle?' Siti shrieked.

Dad chuckled. 'Nope.'

'Why not?'

'Because it will take a lot of money to construct a swimming pool inside the space shuttle. Water will float in microgravity, so an advanced anti-gravity cabin will have to be built, costing tons of money and manpower.'

'But it can be done, right?' Siti ventured.

I shook my head. Everyone wanted some form of paradise on the space shuttle.

'It can be done, but it's not viable. We have to take logistics into account. Cramming a swimming pool into a space shuttle will take up a lot of space. Top priority has to be given to sleepingrooms, kitchen and basic amenities to ensure our survival and comfort in space. You know what I mean, right?'

Siti nodded, the hopeful look in her eyes fading.

Charlie then raised his hand 'How do we cleanse our bladders in space?'

Dad cast a quizzical look at Charlie, his eyebrow arched. 'What do you mean?'

'I mean, how do we pee and poop?' Charlie said bluntly.

I rolled my eyes at Charlie's puerility. Charlie could sometimes sound like a three-year-old baby. At the thought of nature taking its course in space, a knot formed in my stomach. How do we actually pee in space? Would it be the same as peeing on Earth? The sudden, unbidden thought that Charlie's poop might float around and squash me on the face didn't help calm my nerves.

'Oh, don't worry,' Spacey replied. 'The toilets here look pretty much the same as toilets on Earth, but come equipped with a fan vacuum to suck your you-know-what away so there won't be any unnecessary mess.'

OK, that was TMI

Spacey then showed us the way to the nearby toilets, which looked like normal toilets, and once we had relieved ourselves, we finally headed to our own sleeprooms, ready to call it a day.

Charlie, Ken and I changed into our normal clothing and settled in bed.

'I can't stop thinking about the surprise your dad mentioned,' Charlie said. 'What do you think it could be?'

'Maybe there's a library with books and encyclopaedias to keep us occupied when we are bored,' Ken said in a hopeful tone.

Charlie yawned theatrically. 'Ken, this is a space shuttle. Not a school. I'm running out of here if we have to read wordy books.'

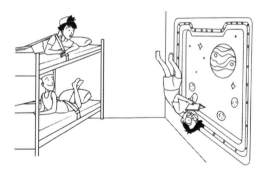

Charlie and I are different from Ken as though we were from different planets. Ken is extremely studious and is big on education, while Charlie and I prefer to do something less mentally strenuous, such as hanging out at the movies, shopping, or going on endless vacations.

'What do you think the surprise is, Robin?' Charlie asked. 'You are your father's son. You should know how he thinks. The apple doesn't fall far from the tree.'

I didn't reply. Instead, I closed my eyes, pretending to be asleep as Charlie and Ken went back and forth about what the surprise could be.

Even though I was supposed to be excited about this space trip, I couldn't help but feel an inexplicable sense of trepidation wash over me, as if some imminent threat was looming over us. Call it my special Robin internal antenna if you will.

It felt like the calm before the storm, when you were blissfully unaware of something ghastly about to happen.

The ominous feeling lingered for a while, and before I knew it, I drifted off into deep slumber.

WHILE I WAS SLEEPING LIKE A BABY . . .

'WAKEY WAKEY UP!!!' boomed Charlie, his shrill voice penetrating into my sleepy head like a knife.

I jerked my bleary eyes open and saw Charlie hovering beside me, his small eyes gleaming. I rubbed my eyes and slowly got out of my bed, a sleepy giddiness still lingering in my head.

'Where's the fire, Charlie?' I huffed, feeling slightly annoyed that he'd roused me from a good sleep. I glanced at Ken, who was perched on his bunk bed on the other side, his hands holding a large book with the title 'ASTRONOMER'S GUIDE TO SPACE' emblazone d on the cover.

It was as though Ken read all the time, even in his sleep—if that was even humanly possible.

'There's no fire, Robin,' Charlie replied good-naturedly, playfully spinning around in mid-air, his handsome face plastered with a wide grin.

'Then what's the rush to wake me up?' I asked.

Charlie chuckled. 'Your father said there will be a "surprise",
remember? I'm just waiting for that surprise, whatever it is. It must
be totally sublime ... coming from your totally phenomenal dad!'

Dad never skimps on surprises; he always goes BIG. One time, he
whisked us away into the ocean in a state-of-the-art submarine,
which was equipped with luxurious features such as an indoor
swimming pool. Another time during my birthday when he flew us
to London, where a giant strawberry cake, as big as the Big Ben,
the clock tower, sat waiting for me in the middle of London Bridge.

My father's surprises are always SUBLIME!!!!

That was why Charlie was probably the first to rouse because he
seemed way more excited than I was, as if the surprise was meant
solely for him.

'I couldn't sleep well thinking about the SURPRISE!' Charlie admitted, his body now drifting past Ken, who was so engrossed in his book that he didn't notice Charlie just inches away from his nose. 'Do you think he has built a space statue in your honor?'

I rolled my eyes. 'I'm not dead, Charlie. Statues are usually built for deceased people who have left behind a great legacy.' I yawned, the desire to sleep tempting me. 'How long did I sleep, Charlie?'

'About six hours, I think. I probably slept around three hours. I hope I don't grow kid wrinkles or something. I read in a health magazine that sleeping less than the required hours can cause premature aging.'

'Charlie, you are beginning to sound like your mom!'

That was something Manda, Botox-obsessed and wrinkle-fearing, would say. Her obsession with skincare must have rubbed off on Charlie in some way.

As Charlie was about to open his mouth to form a reply, the door to our room clunked open, and in came Spacey, Dad, Mom, Alibaba, Manda and the three girls.

Everyone looked like they were going to a jamboree, their faces plastered with excitement.

'Are you guys READY FOR THE SURPRISE???' Dad bellowed jauntily, and everyone began whooping. 'Everyone, follow me.'

'But I need to shower first,' I said, yawning and stretching my arms.

'Yeah,' Charlie said dryly. 'Robin smells like chicken barf.'

'Shut up, Charlie,' I hissed, glaring at Charlie.

After a quick shower at the designated shower cubicle, I joined everyone as we trailed behind my father. We exited through a door into a narrow hall, drifted down the passage, and entered a small, dimly lit chamber with a metallic shelf lining one side of the wall. On the shelf sat what appeared to be dozens of white space helmets. On another side of the wall was circular hatch door, which I thought would lead to another chamber.

'Guys, the moment has come,' Dad said in a slightly breathless voice, his lips turning into a lopsided smile. 'THE SURPRISE IS BEHIND THIS HATCH DOOR.'

Gazing at the hatch door, I wondered what surprise lay beyond. Would there be a statue built in my likeness just as Charlie had mentioned? Nah. If this were true, I'd totally freak out.

'Everyone, don your space helmets,' Dad boomed, gesturing at the space helmets on the shelf.

Everyone gasped, as though the realization was beginning to sink: Why would we need space helmets?

That could only mean one thing . . .

'ARE WE GOING OUT OF HERE TO SPACE???' everyone cried, a mixture of disbelief and excitement in their voices.

Dad nodded, his eyes twinkling. 'Right as rain!'

The entire chamber resounded with whoops and cheers as we float-danced in the air, then proceeded to change into the provided spacesuits from the rack.

'Too bad we left our fashionably customized spacesuits back in our sleeprooms,' Siti lamented. 'The spacesuits provided here are so dull and patternless.'

'Siti,' I said, chuckling, 'we're going to explore space, not doing a fashion show.'

Once everyone was suited up, we hovered close to the hatch, ready to explore the open space.

I couldn't help but feel a prickle of goosebumps at the thought of floating out in the open, in this vast space of darkness.

'CAN WE GO NOW?!' Charlie said impatiently, rubbing his hands in glee.

'Robin, will you do the honors?' Dad said, pointing to the wheel handle of the hatch.

My heart pounded, and I gasped. I couldn't believe that I got to be the first to open the hatch to the infinite world of space!

'It would be my deepest pleasure!!' I trilled, my hands gripping the wheel handle and slowly turning it anti-clockwise until a pop sounded. Taking a deep breath, I thrust the hatch door open, my temples throbbing with feverish excitement.

What I saw before me made my jaw drop, and a feeling of great awe washed over me.

Stretching far and wide was a large expanse of rocky surface, which looked like a giant carpet of powdery dark gray, scattered with rocks, pebbles, boulders, and bowl-shaped cavities. The Moon loomed right in front of our very eyes, so close that I was completey blown away.

Only a one-metre gap stood between our space shuttle and the Moon; that was how close we were! Just one leap forward and we'd be literally on the Moon.

I was so over the Moon!

For a moment, everyone stayed transfixed, heads craning to peek through the open hatch at the spectacular view of the Moon.

Some of us couldn't believe that it was actually the Moon right in front of us. 'IS THAT THE MOON???'

'I'm afraid so,' Dad said jokingly with a good-natured chuckle.

'Mr. Jin, did you just bring us to the Moon????' Charlie asked my father, his eyes bulging out in an almost comical, cartoonish way.

'Of course I did,' Dad chirped, his eyes roaming each and everyone of us. 'I also wanted to gift Robin a special trip to the Moon as a secret birthday surprise!'

I smiled in spite of myself. I was the luckiest boy in the entire galaxy, really.

'THANK YOU, DAD!' I practically squealed. 'THIS IS THE BEST GIFT EVER!!!'

This gift is from both your mom and I,' Dad said, his eyes swiveling to Mom, 'She suggested the Moon trip as part of your birthday surprise, in addition to the space shuttle ride.'

I leapt forward and hugged both Dad and Mom, swept with feelings of euphoria and gratitude. They're both the best parents in the whole wide world.

'Are you guys ready to do your moonwalk?' Mom asked brightly with a wink.

'YES!!!!!' everyone chorused excitedly.

Manda's eyes widened into saucers as she gazed through the open hatch door at the Moon. 'I hope to collect some Moon specimens,' Manda murmured to Alibaba. 'I read in an article that they have rejuvenating properties for the skin.'

I chuckled at Manda's ceaseless anti-aging obsession. Maybe the Moon specimens would turn her into an alien.

Jorge then appeared through the doorway and briefed us on our Moon outing. 'I'll be the group leader of our outing. Due to lower gravity, you can freely float around on the Moon. But please remember to stay close together, don't venture too far from the group, and always stay within sight of one another. There's enough oxygen supply in your spacesuits to last a couple of hours, so you don't have to worry about oxygen depletion. We'll explore the Moon for about an hour . . . '

Once the briefing ended, Siti whipped out her phone camera, took multiple selfies and wefies with us. 'I feel like the Queen of the Moon. Once we return to Earth, I'll post these photos and it will be crazy!'

Siti is an avid social media user, with tens of thousands of followers. She loves posting photos from all our trips, from our first vacation in the Bahamas to an amazing road trip in the heart of Borneo.

'I hope we bump into aliens or something,' Charlie said dryly, giggling. 'But let's hope they won't want to eat us.'

Ken, who was into space and possibly aliens, instantly looked animated like a cartoon character. 'That would be a dream come true. In fact, I wouldn't mind if we discover some new form of life here. This would be the best experience ever.'

I shuddered at the thought of possibly bumping into creatures with eyes as big as saucers and tongues that could turn into sharp edges, ready to saw us off like a chainsaw.

Thanks but no thanks.

Just plainly walking—or catwalking—on the Moon would be just fine.

Through the open hatch door, we leapt from our space shuttle towards the Moon on the other side, our bodies drifting languidly across the small gap as though we were moving clouds.

Once my feet touched the ground of the Moon, a tremble of excitement rippled through me, my heart beating so fast that I could literally faint with the purest of joy.

I had stepped on the Moon!!! Could you seriously believe that???

When everyone had settled on the Moon surface, phone cameras began clicking away, murmurs of awe and excitement rising.

'Siti, capture a video of me moonwalking,' Charlie said jauntily as he started 'catwalking' back and forth as though he was a Moon model.

Siti chuckled, her phone camera aimed at Charlie's exaggerated, shameless moonwalk, which made he look like he had a seizure.

On the Moon, everyone hovered around, drifting up and down, across, and diagonally, marveling and enjoying every moment of it before finally taking a group shot together on the Moon with a self-timed camera on a tripod.

Manda, of course, was busy collecting small pebbles and stuffing them into a small burgundy pouch in the name of youth. Since she and Alibaba couldn't kiss each other on the lips through the space helmets, they kissed anyway, helmet-to-helmet. Would their sloppy kisses ever cease?

As for Chloe, she drifted along the Moon as though she was a goddess from a mythical fable, jotting her observations into a glittery pink notepad, while Ken hovered around with a huge magnifying glass, looking for specimens he could bring back for his personal collection or scientific study.

Siti and Devi took photos together with different poses: somersaults in the air, cartwheels, handstands forward and backward rolls it was definitely easier to do such moves in space due to microgravity.

Mom and Dad drifted a little further away from the rest of us (but not completely out of sight), held hands and marveled at the surroundings around them. What lovey-doveys they were!

I just leave everyone to their business because I had one crucial thing to do: I HAD TO LEAVE MY MARK ON THE MOON.

My heart pounding with excitement, I floated towards a rocky boulder as high as my waist. A crater sat a few feet away. I retrieved a random pebble and started writing on the surface in huge, bold letters:

ROBIN JIN WAS HERE ON THE MOON! DON'T YA EVER FORGET THAT! WITH SO MUCH LOVE, ROBIN!!!!

There, I'd finally made my mark on the Moon, recording my name here for posterity.

'No fair!' Charlie said suddenly, floating down right beside me. 'I need to be next to my best friend!' Instantly, with a pebble in one hand, Charlie started writing his name across the surface next to my name:

CHARLIE KONG IS FOREVER ON THE MOON!!!

I sighed, a wry smile on my face. Did Charlie and I have to do everything together like a pair of inseparable twins, including going to the toilet and dressing in the same clothes?

WHEN CHARLIE INSISTS BEST FRIENDS DO EVERYTHING TOGETHER ...

Can't Charlie give me some space? I felt so suffocated sometimes.

'Charlie,' I said calmly, trying to prevent World War Three. 'You could have written your name at least ten inches away from my spot, you know.'

Charlie screwed up his eyes in horror, his hands pressed against the mouth of his space helmet. 'How could I be so far away from my best friend? I thought we do everything together, right?'

I shook my head incredulously, about to retort, but decided against it. It was my birthday, after all, and I shouldn't be a total scrooge.

'Fine, bestie,' I said, smiling weakly.

I wasn't the only one carving my name on the Moon; everyone else jumped on the bandwagon! Names and messages were scribbled all over the Moon's surface.

I sighed. I thought this was my birthday, and wasn't the birthday boy supposed to have dibs on the Moon? I guess everyone just wanted to share the glory.

But seeing everyone's happy faces, it was indeed a birthday well-celebrated.

'Guess what I wrote?' Chloe said, pointing to a lengthy text, which she had written next to a jagged rock. It looked like she had written a short essay about the Moon titled 'The Wonders of the Moon'. Chloe always scores top marks for her essays in class, and she's easily our English teacher's pet. I swear sometimes she eats textbooks for breakfast.

'Sorry, Chloe,' Charlie yawned, 'but reading essays is the last thing on my mind right now.' Chloe pouted, dragging Siti and Devi to read her written work instead.

After more than an hour on the moon, Dad finally signaled for us to head back to our space shuttle, eliciting groans from us kids as we felt that it was too soon to leave.

I wished I could stay a second longer on the Moon, because I had left my heart here between the craters. How could I leave when this place meant so much to me? Part of me wanted to crawl into the crater and stay on the Moon for as long as I could, but another part of me felt a little eerie staying alone here on this uninhabited Moon, where signs of life were non-existent. It was as though I were in a colossal museum at night, with nobody around except lifeless statues of dead people or fossils of dinosaurs.

Okay, going back to the space shuttle was a better option.

'But before we head back to the space shuttle,' Dad trilled, 'we have one last surprise for you.' Jorge then handed Dad a handheld electronic tablet, and Dad's fingers started tapping away across the screen.

Suddenly, a red-colored drone, shaped like a space saucer, whirred out of the doorway of our space shuttle and headed towards us.

'WHAT'S THAT?!!!' my friends and I shouted simultaneously, transfixed by the emergence of the floating drone.

'This is a satellite-enabled drone that will broadcast live video to the entire world,' Dad said, smiling smugly. 'It will shoot a live video of all of us, broadcasting it to all the international cable TVs, which have received a hefty payment from me in order for this feat to happen.'

I gasped incredulously. WE WERE ON LIVE TV NOW???? OH MY GOD!!!!

Not only had I walked the Moon, but my face would be broadcast live to millions of people across the globe. How sublime was that!

'Every top news cable will air this,' Mom chipped in, 'so we're going to do something special.'

Out of the blue, suddenly, everyone began forming a circle around me as if I were some kind of a new alien creature.

What on earth—or moon—were they doing? They were not planning on sacrificng me to the moon goddess, right?

Next second, everyone broke into a birthday song, clapping and cheering jauntily: 'HAPPY BIRTHDAY TO YOU, HAPPY BIRTHDAY TO ROBIN...'

As everyone was singing, the drone hovered above our heads, its camera aimed at us, capturing this amazing occasion on live video!

Tears of joy streamed down my cheeks, and I felt like I could just die and go straight to heaven It appeared that everyone was in on this birthday song surprise! They must have secretly planned this together in advance.

It was most likely Dad's idea, as he always had a wild imagination when it came to surprises.

When the birthday song finally ended, Charlie was playful enough to improvise by singing in his off-pitch voice, 'Happy birthday to you, Robin ... you were born in the zoo ...'

'Shut up, Charlie,' I said, but couldn't help but laugh.

'Livestream has just ended,' Dad said as we watched the drone float back into the spaceship. 'Millions of people have tuned in to your birthday celebration on the Moon. I'm pretty sure your social media will be flooded with comments tomorrow.'

'Oh, Dad, I still can't believe this is happening,' I choked up, in complete disbelief that my birthday was celebrated in style on the moon, and then I turned to look at all my friends. 'Thank you, everyone. I'm deeply touched.'

A magnificent-looking birthday cake floated right in front of me, and my happiness barometre went off the charts.

Charlie turned to Alibaba. 'Stepdaddy,' Charlie said, tugging at Alibaba's sleeve. 'Can I have a party on the Moon for my birthday next year?'

'Yes, you can,' Alibaba said with a slight smirk. 'I will have an artificial moon built in our backyard, equipped with other planetary accessories.'

Charlie groaned theatrically, and everyone laughed in amusement.

After having spent a fruitful time on the Moon, we finally returned to our space shuttle and headed to the tiny space kitchen so we could all have a slice of my birthday cake, We also helped ourselved to pre-packed food in plastic wraps, which could be eaten by just tearing off the seals, and there was also a special oven to heat a up food.

After a hearty meal, everyone returned to their own sleeprooms, and Charlie, Ken and I settled ourselves comfortably in our own bed.

'Good night, my beloved friends,' Ken said with a yawn, strapping himself to his bed.

'Is it really night?' Charlie said. 'I can't really tell. Is there day or night in space? I mean, it's constantly dark, right? We're in space, hello?'

I chuckled. 'Just go to sleep, Charlie.'

Charlie's words lingered in my head, and I started thinking about sunny beaches, clear blue skies, rolling hills, and fresh air. I kind of missed Earth a little, to be honest. Even though space was totally sublime, Earth was where my heart really belonged.

I flicked the switch on the wall beside my bed, and instantly, the room lights dimmed.

From my bed, I could see that Ken was already asleep on his bunk bed on the other side; I couldn't see what Charlie was doing as he was below me.

I closed my eyes and turned on my side, ready to sleep.

Seconds later, I could hear Charlie snoring like a rumbling truck, and I sighed, wondering if I'd be able to sleep. Too bad microgravity couldn't lift noises away.

I turned to look at Ken, who was sleeping beatifically like Sleeping Beauty, unaffected by Charlie's snoring. How could Ken sleep through all that noise? He was one heavy sleeper, I'll give him that.

If only I had Ken's Sleeping Beauty ability, because I couldn't sleep through Charlie's noisy 'orchestra'. I tossed and turned in my bed, feeling as though I was suffering terrible insomnia.

After several failed attempts at trying to sleep, I decided to get out of bed, unstrapped myself and floated towards the door. Maybe I could explore the space shuttle while everyone was asleep. Who knew. I might stumble on something interesting...

My heart pounding, I floated out the door and down a narrow passageway, which was lined with metallic doors on either side, wondering what lay beyond those doors. Everyone had been so busy with my moon outing birthday surprise that we didn't really have the time to explore every inch of the space shuttle.

One particular door towards the end, which was creamy white and emblazoned all over with black zigzag patterns, caught my eye. Curious, I floated towards the strange-looking door, slowly unlatched it, then opened it.

What could lay beyond this door?

My stomach clenched as I took in the sight before me: beyond the door was a tiny chamber, which was utterly bare and lined with a few glass circular windows offering a glimpse of space. A long red belt, which was wound up like a fire hose, was attached to one side of the door, and hooked to the other side of the silvery walls was a pair of spacesuits, complete with helmets.

What was the long red belt used for? And why were there two spacesuits inside this strange room?

I floated towards the centre of the desolate chamber, a strange sense of trepidation washing over me.

'WHAT ARE YOU DOING HERE???!!!' a familiar high-pitched voice boomed behind me.

I stopped midway and jerked around. 'Charlie!!!!!' I cried incredulously. 'I thought you were sleeping. You were snoring like World War Six or something.'

'I do not!' Charlie retorted, floating towards me, a frown plastered on his face. 'Are my snores that bad, seriously?'

'Forget your bad snores. What are you doing here???'

'I woke up from this awfully terrible dream,' Charlie said, shivering. 'I don't know, Robin, but I don't usually get bad dreams like this. It could be a sign from the universe . . .'

Seeing the slight terror in Charlie's eyes sent chills down my spine. Was he being real, or was he pulling my leg?

'Dream? What kind of dream?' I asked.

'I dreamt I was in total darkness ... with no way out,' Charlie answered with a deep gulp. 'I felt so lost ... as though I was in a never-ending maze.'

'Oh, Charlie,' I huffed, crossing my arms over my chest. 'It's just a bad dream. It's not going to happen, okay?'

Charlie's face remained so serious that I actually believed him for once, and I began feeling goosebumps prickling across my flesh. I didn't feel at ease anymore. It was probably better for us if we headed back to our sleeproom now.

'Let's go back to our sleeproom,' I said, making my way towards the door.

When I saw that the door was completely shut, my jaw dropped. I didn't recall ever closing the door. Wait. Did Charlie close the door behind him when he entered the chamber?

Perhaps the door had automatically shut itself, and needed to be manually reopened. So I floated right in front of the door and tried to open it, but it WOULDN'T BUDGE!

'The door's not opening!!!!!' I cried, panic rising within me.

'WHAT?!' Charlie squeaked. 'Are you kidding? Here, let me try.' He hurtled towards the door, turned the doorknob and pushed it, but still, it wouldn't budge. 'Oh my God! We're locked inside!'

'Do not panic yet,' I said, even though I felt far from calm. 'Where there's a way in, there's definitely a way out!'

Charlie rolled his eyes. 'There's only one door in this chamber! There's no other way out of here!'

I started hyperventilating, my heart pounding so hard that it felt like it felt like it would rupture my rib cage my rib cage.

'Charlie, QUIET!' I cried, refusing to hear the negative thoughts from Charlie. My eyes began darting everywhere inside the chamber for a possible way out. 'There has to be something in here to help us get out ...'

'How about we scream for HELP?' Charlie suggested.

We started screaming like a pack of wild hyenas, slamming our fists against the metallic door, but it of no use, because it seemed the entire chamber was soundproof.

Out of the corner of my eye, on the other side of the wall, I spotted a tiny rectangular control panel, which had buttons and dial knobs, and I was filled with a sudden ray of hope, hoping that the control panel might somehow unlock the door.

Immediately, I zoomed towards the control panel and stared at the buttons, a frown on my face. What did these buttons do? What if we press the wrong ones?

When Charlie realized that there was a control panel, he was ecstatic. 'Yes! Yes!' Charlie cried, hovering right beside me and staring intently at the control panel. 'We're going to get out of here soon! We just need to press the right buttons.'

'But which buttons should we press?' I asked, my eyebrows furrowed. 'There are no labels or any clear indication.'

'Who cares?!' Charlie retorted, recklessly punching all the buttons in wild sweeping motions.

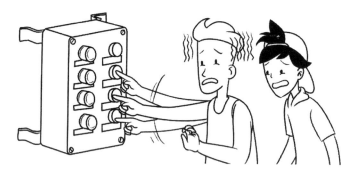

'CHARLIE, ARE YOU NUTS?!' I cried, deeply alarmed by Charlie's recklessness. 'Don't do that.'

But it was too late. After Charlie had sloppily pressed all the buttons on the control panel, a sudden, booming swoosh could be heard, like the sound of gas being released.

'Wh-what's g-going on?' Charlie asked fearful tone, his head swiveling around in every direction.

I jerked around, floated towards the door, and tried opening the door once more, but my heart sank when the door remained stationary. Would we ever get out of here???

And what was that swooshing sound we'd heard just moments ago?

Charlie also tried his luck with the door. 'The door won't budge!' Charlie grunted, both hands yanking the doorknob with excessive force.

Then all of a sudden, the entire chamber rattled and shook violently, sending Charlie and I knocking into each other.

'WHAT'S GOING ON?' Charlie demanded, groaning in pain.

'I DON'T KNOW!' I cried, my head throbbing in pain as the chamber continued shaking mysteriously.

Next second, after rattling for a brief moment, the entire chamber seemed to thrust upwards at lightning speed, as though it was a rocket being launched. I felt like I was being catapulted heavenward, my whole body racked with pain at the overwhelming, dizzying sensation.

Screams ripped the air as the entire chamber shot upwards like a cannonball, dragging both Charlie and I along with it. The chamber ascended speedily for several moments, then came to a grinding halt, which made Charlie and I bump heads painfully.

Charlie and I groaned in distress, trying to find our bearings and make sense of the strange deviation.

'What just happened?' Charlie demanded tremulously, his bloodshot eyes widening. 'I almost broke every bone in my body. It felt like we were on a wild roller-coaster ride! What on earth—I mean space—was all that???'

'I-I h-have n-no idea,' I spluttered, straining against the throbbing pain in my body as I made my way towards the nearest window. 'It felt like the whole room was moving . . .'

I reached the glass-paneled window, peered out, then screamed my lungs out, 'NOOOOOOOOOOOOOOOOOOOO!!!!'

'What's going on????' Charlie asked in deep concern, dashing to my side. He followed my gaze, and when he saw what I saw, he erupted into a bloodcurdling scream.

'IS THAT OUR SPACESHIP????!!!' Charlie cried incredulously, his face completely ashen.

Out the window in the far distance, I saw our space shuttle, Shuttle Robin, becoming a smaller and smaller dot as it floated further and further away from Charlie and I. I watched in terror, realizing that we had been separated from all our family and friends!

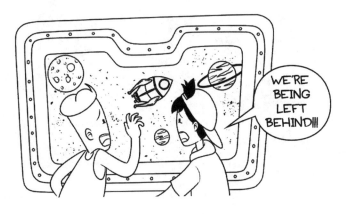

DID OUR CHAMBER JUST GET DETACHED FROM THE REST OF THE SPACE SHUTTLE??????

Charlie's clammy hands gripped mine, and he looked like he was about to throw up. 'Robin, d-do y-you know what I think?' Charlie stammered, a petrified look plastered across his sweaty face. 'I reckon that this entire chamber, which we're inside right now, is some kind of an escape pod, which ejects from the space shuttle during an emergency! I- I ...,' Charlie paused, close to tears, 'I think I might have pressed the wrong button ... the EJECT button!'

Apoplectic with rage, I smacked Charlie up and down. This 'this was all Charlie's fault! Because of his recklessness, we were stuck in this escape pod, which was floating aimlessly away from our space shuttle and our family and friends, away from Earth!

WERE WE GOING TO BE LOST IN SPACE FOREVER????

CHARLIE, THIS IS ALL YOUR FAULT! NOW WE'RE GOING TO BE LOST IN SPACE!

WOULD ANYONE EVEN KNOW CHARLIE AND I WERE OUT HERE, DRIFTING FURTHER AND FURTHER AWAY FROM THE WORLD, A MERE SMALL DOT IN THIS INFINITE DARK FABRIC?

The feelings of anxiety and fear were so overwhelming that I broke down in tears, and I flicked a teary-eyed gaze out the small glass window, at nothing but pure solitary darkness, my hope of being rescued dashed.

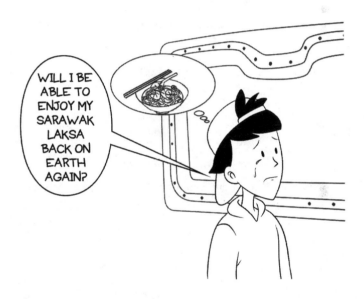

AFTER AN HOUR HAD PASSED . . .

'Robin, HOW LONG ARE YOU GOING TO CRY????' Charlie asked, floating above me like the Grim Reaper about to take my lifeless soul.

I wiped away the tear stains from my face, sniffling continuously, my nose feeling so clogged up. I'd cried so hard that I didn't think there were any tears left in my tear ducts.

I then glanced up at Charlie, my legs crossed in mid-air. 'Charlie, what should we do now? We're probably miles away from our family and friends. We will probably never ever see them—'

'STOP SAYING THAT, ROBIN!' Charlie snapped, sidling up beside me and shaking some sense into me. 'You're supposed to be the positive one, not me! We need to stay calm and focused! Help will be here!' But there was a slight quiver at his last word, with Charlie's forced confident look faltering.

ROBIN, YOU CRY MORE THAN A BABY.

My tears flowed again. I'd always been the one with a more positive mindset than Charlie, but now that we were 'literally' lost in space, my spirits were completely down, with a hopeless sense that we would never make out of this alive.

Hovering close to the window, Charlie and I fixed our dejected gazes at the vast expanse of darkness, which was sprinkled with small dots of stars; Our space shuttle was not even visible anymore, which had probably floated away far out of reach.

'I can't see our space shuttle anywhere!' Charlie squaked, his eyes darting back and forth everywhere through the window. 'Do-do you-you think they're … looking for us?'

A ray of hope, so flimsy that it was barely visible, filled me. I was pretty sure that everyone would, sooner or later, discover that we were missing and then come looking for us. Dad would send out a search and rescue team, and help would soon be on the way.

Or maybe not, because space was this ginormous, infinite universe, and it was not the same as Earth, where you could easily locate people via GPS or CCTVs. Looking for us in space would be like looking for a needle in a haystack.

WOULD WE EVER BE FOUND?????

'C-Charlie...' I choked back tears, 'I-I don't know. I-I really don't know. I just pray that they'll come looking for us.' I'd never prayed so hard in my life, my hands clasped tight in prayer as I desperately begged help from every God in the universe.

'Robin,' Charlie began with a nervous edge in his voice, 'do you realize that our chamber is constantly moving?'

A deep gulp went down my throat. Charlie was right. I could feel the continuous motion of the entire chamber, which drifted across space, further and further away from Earth.

A sudden, petrifying thought struck my mind: Would we be sucked into a black hole somewhere and be banished forever?

Or would we end up on a new planet somewhere in the galaxy, which had aliens waiting to eat our heads off???

Shivers ran down my spine as the horrible thoughts raced through my head.

'Yes,' I admitted bleakly, 'I can feel our chamber constantly moving, slowly but surely.'

'Do you think we can somehow steer this chamber back to our space shuttle?' Charlie said in a hopeful tone.

Our eyes began wandering over every inch of the chamber, searching for any steering wheels that could navigate us in the opposite direction, towards Shuttle Robin, where our family and friends were.

When I realized that there was none, the knots in my stomach tightened severely.

Who built this STUPID chamber, without the common sense to equip it with a steering wheel so it could be driven around? Were Charlie and I supposed to be trapped here for eternity like lab mice?

'Wait!' Charlie cried abruptly, startling me. 'I think I may have spotted something!' Charlie hurtled his way towards a tiny silver lever, which protruded from the furthest end of the wall, looking so small eye that it would take a sharp eye to notice it. 'What is this lever for?'

I floated towards Charlie and joined him near the lever, my heart pounding as a ray of hope surged through me. Could this lever be useful? Maybe it could somehow steer us back to our space shuttle.

'I have no idea,' I said, slowly fingering the lever, hoping that this would be the answer to our prayers.

'I'm going to pull it,' Charlie said quickly, his hand reaching for it.

'WAIT!!!!' I cried immediately, my stomach clenching so hard that I could feel my intestines twisting inside. Why did I have such a terrible feeling about this? But if we didn't try it, we would never know, right? After all, we were running out of options.

IT WAS EITHER PULL THE LEVER OR ROT INSIDE HERE FOREVER!

'You don't want me to pull the lever?' Charlie croaked.

'J-just ... pull it,' I said tentatively, my lower lip trembling.

With bated breath, Charlie finally jerked the lever down with his hand.

All of a sudden, a computerized voice boomed in the air, 'Door will open in twenty seconds . . . Door will open in twenty seconds . . . '

Charlie chuckled wryly. 'I can't believe it! This is the lever that opens the door! We're going to be free!' Charlie kissed the lever several times as though it was his angel sent from heaven.

A sudden epiphany struck me, and my blood ran cold.

'Charlie, you spoke too soon!' I cried, my hands pressed against my cheeks. 'Do you know what's going to happen to us??? We're detached from our space shuttle, remember? When that door opens, we'll be exposed to the harsh elements of space! No oxygen! We're doomed!'

Charlie's eyes bulged in horror. 'Oh my God! I never thought about that at all! What are we going to do???'

My heart thumped wildly and my eyes darted to the pair of spacesuits on the wall. 'Hurry! We need to wear those spacesuits before the door opens!'

I immediately grabbed Charlie's arm, and together, we scrambled towards the spacesuits, suited up and strapped on the helmets.

All of a sudden, a deafening, bursting sound erupted, as though something had been ripped apart, followed quickly by a strong whooshing noise.

'AHHHHHHHHHHHHHHH!' Charlie and I screamed, our eyes darting upwards to where the sound came from.

There was a wide, gaping hole above us, giving us unobstructed view of space; the entire ceiling had been ripped apart, completely gone! The huge gap, where the ceiling had once been, stood dangerously between us and the open space!

I wailed in terror at the dark gaping hole, where the door had once stood. The lever, which could have had some faulty wiring, must have caused the ceiling to burst when it should have opened the door instead.

And that was not the worst of it. A strong, sucking force was pulling us upwards like a vacuum cleaner, towards the gaping hole! Instinctively, I fumbled for the nearest object I could find, and clung onto a rudder on the wall inches away from me, my whole body upside down as my legs were pulled, almost magnetically, upwards, while my hands held on to the rudder.

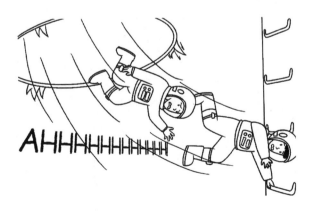

Unfortunately, for Charlie, before he could grab hold of anything, his entire body had been sucked upward and out into space, his blood-curdling scream ringing in the air.

'ROBIN, HELPPPPPPPPPPPI!'

I watched, helplessly, in terror, as Charlie hurtled across space above me like a cannonball, his limbs flailing violently, and as he spiraled further and further away from me into the void, his entire body shrinking.

My heart leapt to my throat when I saw Charlie's helmet slip off from his head and float away from him. Charlie flailed helplessly around above me, his face twisting in agony, suddenly deprived of oxygen. He was not going to make it without oxygen! He only had mere seconds to live!

'CHARLIE!!!!' I cried, my mind racing, as I darted my eyes around for ways to save Charlie.

I saw the long red winding belt next to the door, and, instinctively, I sprang from the rudder towards the belt, grabbed and unlooped it, then strapped it tight around my waist so it would anchor me back to the chamber. That probably what it was used for.

I then catapulted myself upwards through the gaping ceiling hole and out into space, the belt holding me securely in place so I wouldn't venture off course.

I now had only seconds to spare, as I vaguely recalled Ken telling me once that a person had less than a minute to live if he was exposed to space without oxygen.

'Charlie, I'm coming for you!' I bellowed. I hurtled towards Charlie's floating helmet, grabbed it and scrambled right next to Charlie, just as the anchoring belt had stretched to its limit.

WOULD I MAKE IT IN TIME???

Charlie blanched, his bloodshot eyes bulging in terror and his limbs flailing as he struggled for air; it broke my heart to see Charlie in such a miserable state, as he had always been the cheerful, silly type.

A second later, I quickly plopped the space helmet onto Charlie's head and held onto him tightly so he would stop drifting away.

Charlie suddenly stopped moving about, his eyes closed. My stomach clenched. Wait. Was I too late???

I gazed, intently and anxiously, at Charlie's motionless face.

'No, Charlie!!!' I cried, my eyes welling up. 'Please don't die on me!'

I held my lifeless best friend in my arms, tears trickling down my cheeks, gazing at his face. Moments later, strangely, the paleness on his face gradually faded into a healthier shade, and before I knew it, his bleary eyes fluttered open.

CHARLIE MADE IT!

A relieved smile broke on my lips.

'Wh-what j-j-just h-happened?' Charlie spluttered, his eyes flitting open repeatedly as if alien insects were crawling inside his sockets.

'You almost died!' I said, hugging Charlie so tight that I never wanted to ever let him go. My best friend. My confidant. Who else could I turn to for advice on fine dining or the hottest vacation spots in the world if Charlie was permanently gone from this world—I mean—space?

Charlie's confused expression turned to realization as he slowly recalled everything. 'Oh my God! Oh my God! Now I remember! I was sucked out into space without any space helmet on! I ALMOST MET MY CREATOR!!!'

I grinned in spite of myself. This was the Charlie I missed, the dramatic boy who always had the wrong things to say.

Charlie winced as I hugged him. 'Why are you holding onto me like we are a married couple?'

'Two reasons,' I said, not sure whether to strangle Charlie for being the most annoying boy in the universe. 'I'm so glad you're alive, and the feeling of losing you forever was just too overwhelming for me. Second . . . I have to hold you like an anchor so you won't float away.' I gave him a wry smile. 'Would you have preferred if I let you go and watch you float into space?'

Charlie flashed me a mischievous grin, chuckling. 'Just admit that you l-o-v-e me.'

I rolled my eyes, utterly tempted to release my grip on him and let him float away into oblivion. But what kind of friend would I be if I did that?

'Come on, let's make our way back into the chamber,' I said, my hands gripping the long belt, which was anchored directly to the chamber floating below us. 'Hold onto me, Charlie.'

As Charlie clung to me, I grabbed the belt in both fists and started tugging my way towards the chamber. Then, just as we were almost reaching the chamber, a mere metre away, the sound of a sharp snap pierced the air.

'NOOOOOOOOOOOOO!!!!!' Charlie and I both cried when the belt suddenly snapped, thrusting us backward in the opposite direction.

'Why do accidents like this keep happening to us???' Charlie shrieked, his arms still wrapped around me. 'Is the whole universe conspiring against us?'

My heart was pounding so hard against my rib cage that my insides felt like they were going to implode.

We were certainly going to be lost in space for good, with no one around to help us. The feeling of unimaginable fear gripped me at the thought of imminent death in space, in a place far away from home. Nobody would be able to lay flower wreaths at our graveyards, because there were no graveyards in space!

Oh my God! How did I get sucked into such deeply morbid thoughts?

As I gazed blankly into the dark void, I felt that all hope was lost. Charlie and I were now floating haphazardly in space, mere tiny dots in this gargantuan expanse of infinity.

'Oh, Robin,' Charlie cried, sobbing uncontrollably. 'What should be do?'

I felt a deep pit in my stomach. There was nothing we could do, but wait for our death. Our oxygen levels would deplete soon, and then, there was nothing much left that we could do.

Then, out of the corner of my eye, I thought I saw something vaguely familiar in the distance, probably about less than a mile away. When I saw what it was , my heart began to swell a little.

'Charlie, is that the ... MOON????!!!!' I cried, transfixed by the sight of what appeared to be the moon, which had a rocky surface, coated with powdery dark gray.

'IT'S THE MOON, ALRIGHT!' Charlie whooped, pumping his fist triumphantly.

We had been such a pair of nervous wrecks that we hadn't even noticed that the Moon was just a stone's throw away from us all this while. Your sense of orientation can get a little haywire when you are in space.

With renewed hope, Charlie and I scrambled over towards the Moon, our hands flailing around as though we were swimming. It took several moments before we finally reached the Moon's surface, our faces brightening as our feet touched the pebble-scattered surface of the Moon.

I turned to Charlie, whose elated expression suddenly turned grim.

'What's wrong, Charlie?' I asked, patting him on the shoulder. 'Aren't you glad we reached the Moon? It's better than floating aimlessly in space, right?'

'So what if we landed on the Moon?' Charlie said grumpily, his eyes filled with sadness. 'Nobody's going to find us. Ever. We're going to die here on the Moon.'

My heart sank. Charlie was right. It was too soon to celebrate. Even though we were now on the Moon, what could we actually do? There was no oxygen on the Moon, and we wouldn't be able to survive here long-term.

Charlie then floated over a bowl-shaped cavity and descended into it, his body curled into a little ball of misery. I floated down and joined him, sitting beside him and staring blankly into space.

'Robin . . . ,' Charlie said shakily, choking back tears. 'We probably won't make it. Let's just face the facts rather than seeing things through rose-tinted glasses. No humans can survive in space without oxygen. Our space helmets are going to run out of oxygen, you know.'

I winced. I couldn't believe that Charlie would give up easily like this, but deep in my heart, I knew that he was right.

'Robin, I'm so sorry for the things I did in the past to annoy you,' Charlie said apologetically, glancing at me with a contrite look on his face. 'I actually love to tease you. That's because I really like you . . . as my best friend.'

I was touched by Charlie's vulnerability, which he didn't show very often, and it made me a little teary.

'It's true that you annoy me to the max, Charlie,' I sniffled, a weak smile on my face. 'But that's what best friends are for, right? We annoy each other at times, but we also bring out the best in each other. Charlie Kong, I could never ask for a better friend than you,' I then paused, with a melancholic smile, 'and Ken too, of course. You two bring a balance to my unpredictable, extravagant life!'

'And vice versa,' Charlie said, his lips beginning to curve with a tiny smile, a little teary-eyed. 'You are the greatest friend in the world, Robin Jin. Sometimes, I wish I could have your magnificent wardrobe. You have a great sense of style, you know.'

We both laughed at the fact that Charlie thought I had a great sense of style. Personally, for me, the most important thing is to be yourself, and you will shine through no matter what. No amount of great clothing can dictate your personality and style.

'Charlie,' I began tentatively, feeling slightly bold, 'since we're both out here alone awaiting our doom, do you have any confession to make?' After all, what did we have to lose? We weren't going to make it out of here alive, so it didn't matter anymore if we revealed our deepest secrets.

'I-I... hate my stepfather,' Charlie choked up, his eyes darkening slightly.

I gasped, blinking. I had no idea that Charlie despised Alibaba, because they had always seemed so cozy together, like father and son. They had even gone on countless vacations, and it was strange to think that Charlie could hate Alibaba. It was a total revelation for me.

'But why?' I asked, 'I thought you liked him?'

Charlie gazed forlornly upwards into the eternal night, one lone tear trickling own his cheek, as though he'd kept that tear locked up in a . . . in a special place in his tear duct for so long.

'The truth is . . . ,' Charlie sniffled, 'I miss my real father.'

My jaw dropped. Charlie rarely mentioned his real father. In fact, he hated talking about his biological father, who was involved in a messy divorce with his mom more than four years ago.

'Have you ever tried contacting him?' I asked.

Charlie finally let his emotions get the best of him. Trembling uncontrollably, he broke into tears, his bleary eyes filled with a range of emotions: longing, anger, and sadness.

'I-I ... want to,' Charlie said, tears welling in his eyes. 'but I hate him for leaving Mom and me, and I can't help but wonder sometimes how he's doing with his new family in China.'

I sighed, holding Charlie's hand empathetically. When Charlie's father had married a Chinese model, they recolated to Shanghai to start a new family. I couldn't imagine the pain Charlie must have felt when his father had made that dreadful decision.

'I hate him for causing me so much pain,' Charlie said, 'but I really miss him a lot that it hurts sometimes.'

With my hands outstretched, I gave Charlie a big hug, wanting him to know that I would be there for him as a friend.

Who would have ever thought that Charlie and I would get so mushy and vulnerable up here on the Moon? It was the last thing I expected, considering that Charlie was really private about his feelings, especially when it concerned his biological father.

Well, I always believe that things happen for a reason, and although I wasn't sure what the reason was that Charlie and I were put in such a tight spot, it was refreshing to see this vulnerable side of Charlie, who had always tried to conceal his true self by showing only the best part of himself.

'But why do you hate Alibaba too?' I asked softly. 'You always seemed to like him so much.'

'That's because I 'tried' to like him,' Charlie said with a heavy sigh. 'I felt this deep void in my heart when my biologicl father left, so when Alibaba came into my life, I thought he would take my father's place and erase that pain. But boy, I was so wrong. It had been a pretense all along,' Charlie paused, absent-mindedly flicking a few moon pebbles off the ground, which floated upwards in front of him, 'but the truth was, I really need my father. I miss him. And I keep asking myself ... does he miss me as well? Is he thinking of me all the way in China? Or has he forgotten about me?'

Charlie's confession tugged at my heartstrings, and I held his hand in mine, looking him in the eye. 'Charlie, listen . . . I hadn't expected our talk would go so deep like this . . . but I'm so glad you shared because I'd have never known about your hidden misery.' I choked up a little, getting a little teary. 'Funny how things unfold when you least expect them to, right? And I can assure you that your father loves and misses you lot.'

Charlie's eyes glistened with slight hope. 'You really think so?'

I nodded. 'I believe that with all my heart. He probably wants to see you again, but maybe he's afraid that he'll hurt you further. He knows that you hate him so much because of the divorce, so probably, he has been holding back from trying to see you.'

Charlie sniffled, staring blankly into space. 'I don't know . . . if I'll ever forgive my dad, Robin.'

'It takes great strength to forgive, Charlie.'

I DON'T KNOW IF I'LL EVER FORGIVE MY DAD ... BUT I'LL TRY.

Okay, I knew I sounded strange like a preacher, which was something out of character for me. Maybe because I was on the verge of death, all the wisdom, which had been suppressed within me, came floating up unexpectedly.

'Thank you for your nugget of wisdom, Robin,' Charlie said, looking slightly relieved. 'You know what? If we ever get back to Earth, the first thing I will do is to find my biological father and be reunited with him.'

But deep down inside, I had a feeling that that wasn't going to happen, because our death clock was ticking away here on the Moon. We would never make it back to Earth.

'Robin!' Charlie suddenly cried, startling me. 'WH-WHAT IS THAT TH-THING?!'

I immediately followed Charlie's wide-eyed gaze and gasped when I saw a silvery cone-shaped space shuttle, about as high as a five-storey apartment, approaching us. A sense of foreboding washed over me. The strange-looking space shuttle had bright, circular orange lights, which were fixed in a complete circle around its body like a beaded necklace, and close to the the peak was a weird crest, which looked like an eye with foreign symbols scattered around its iris.

WHAT IN THE WORLD WAS THAT THING???

'It's come to rescue us!' Charlie cried joyously, looking extremely relieved and floating upwards from the cavity, ready to head towards the strange space shuttle, which had landed on the Moon's surface.

I tugged at Charlie's arm, trying to stall him. 'But Charlie, don't you think it looks like a strange space shuttle? I've never seen anything quite like it.'

THAT EYE SYMBOL GIVES ME THE CREEPS!

'Who cares, Robin?' Charlie snapped, pushing my arm away. 'Never look a gift horse in the mouth.' Without another word, Charlie jerked around and scrambled over towards the cone-shaped space shuttle, leaving me behind as I pondered my options: follow Charlie or stay behind.

I watched as Charlie hovered close to the space shuttle, which seemed to have no door at all. How was a person supposed to enter, if there wasn't any doorway?

'HELP US!' Charlie cried, circling the space shuttle a few times. 'We're stuck here on the Moon. We need help! Is anybody in there?'

A deep gulp went down my throat, as goosebumps prickled across my flesh. Why did I have such a horrid feeling about this?

As Charlie pounded against the space shuttle with his fists, his eyes filled with desperation. I slowly made my way over towards Charlie with a nagging feeling inside me.

Suddenly, the top part of the space shuttle swooshed upward, spinning endlessly like a saucer with tawny lights spilling downward from it. It spiralled higher and higher, completely detached from the rest of its body; it looked to me like a large slice of metallic pizza spinning around in the air.

Charlie cowered at the sight of the spinning saucer and moved slightly backwards, his eyes filled with fear. 'W-what is th-that thing?!'

Before I could form a response, the rapidly spinning saucer inclined towards Charlie, bathing him completely in light, and next second, Charlie let out a shrill scream of terror when his whole body was sucked toward the lights like a magnet. Charlie had his entire back pinned to the underside of the saucer, which looked like the flat surface of an LED panel light.

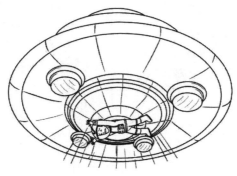

'HELP!' Charlie cried, his spread-eagled limbs unable to move, as though every inch had been pinned. 'What is happening to me?!'

'CHARLIE!' I wailed, my heart ricoheting in my chest. I tried to edge my way towards Charlie, but froze when I saw the terrifying manner in which Charlie was being held captive by the spinning saucer. Would I dare go near and probably suffer the same fate as Charlie?

'ROBIN!' Charlie's haunting cries pierced the air, and unable to see my best friend in pain much longer, I leapt towards Charlie and stretched my arms out, trying to pull Charlie off the spinning saucer, which was holding him like a magnet to a refrigerator.

But before I could even reach my hands towards Charlie, I instantly felt a violent, sucking sensation, which pulled me towards the lights, and eventually, I ended up being pinned, on my back, onto the underside, together with Charlie.

Charlie and I, could do nothing but scream continuously in terror, fixed to the spot as though our limbs were fastened to the surface with nails.

'I'm so DIZZY!' Charlie shrieked.

Still screaming, I tried to sneak a glance at Charlie, but the continual spinning of the saucer was making me extremely giddy and nauseous. I was on the verge of throwing up.

Suddenly, I felt myself being thrust downward fast, as though I was in a lift that was plunging at high speed, then felt my back detach from the saucer's underside, falling downward for several seconds before landing on a cold floor with a loud thud, followed by the sound of a sharp click, like the sound of a padlock being locked.

Groaning in pain on the floor, I twisted and turned, rolling my body onto my back, and scrambled slowly to my feet.

What in the world—I mean space—was going on???

I tilted my head towards Charlie, who was also scrambling to his feet, whimpering in pain, then jerked my gaze upwards at the ceiling, which looked like the underside of the saucer, with its lights dimmed to a large extent, by now. Taking a few moments to compose myself, I began to realize the underside of the saucer, which Charlie and I had been pinned onto, had swooped downwards and capped the space shuttle like a roof, back to the same state it was when we had first seen it emerge. It released Charlie and I from its magnetic grip, causing both of us to fall onto the floor ... inside this STRANGE space shuttle!

It could be DANGEROUS, for all I knew. Who owned this space shuttle? It seemed to have technological capabilities beyond our years.

'R-robin,' Charlie spluttered, and I immediately turned to look at him, a feeling of apprehension sweeping over me. 'Wh-where are we?'

I scurried over to Charlie, wrapped my arms tightly around him, and together, we both scanned our new, foreign surroundings.

We were standing on a circular metallic floor, which was lined at the outermost edge with what seemed to be ancient-looking runes, and towards the centre, where we were standing, was a huge eye symbol, looking exactly like the one we saw on the exterior of the space shuttle.

Around us, the doorless walls curved inwards, as though we were inside a half-sphere, but there was nothing on these walls except steely grey; we were inside an ominously barren room, which was partially lit by the dim lights overhead.

I took a deep gulp as my eyes roamed over the foreign place, feeling as though I was trapped inside a prison.

'Charlie,' I began shakily, 'I–I . . . seriously have no idea where we are. I don't know why, but I don't think we're safe . . . it's just a nagging feeling I have . . .'

'Not safe?' Charlie snapped, but the fear grew in his eyes. 'But how come? I thought we were being rescued?'

I sighed wearily. 'Charlie, think hard. Do you think being sucked onto strange, spinning saucers and then thrashed into this desolate place is called 'being rescued'?'

Charlie gasped, looking completely petrified. 'I-I don't think so . . . so WHAT is this thing we're in???'

Both Charlie and I swiveled our heads around fast, as though something forbidding would emerge any second.

Then, suddenly, the entire rattled slightly as though there was a mini earthquake, and towards our left side, the outline of a door suddenly appeared on the doorless walls. The door took form and slid open to one side, revealing a bright doorway, which was illuminated by a strong light behind it.

I heard footsteps coming from behind the doorway, and immediately, my heart raced. What was beyond that doorway? Would we come face to face with something unimaginably horrid and dangerous?

Charlie gripped my hand tightly, and I could feel his nervous energy rubbing off on me. I froze, my eyes fixed on the doorway, waiting for someone, or probably 'something', to emerge.

'Robin, who do you think is going to come out of that doorway?' Charlie asked, his voice edged with absolute panic.

We didn't have to wait long. Next second, a figure emerged at the doorway, a dark silhoutte against the glaring light behind it, and as it stepped out of the doorway in front of us in clear view, my jaw dropped in deep terror!

An eyeless creature, which had a teardrop-shaped face and long snake-like limbs protruding out of its steely blue body shaped like a big carrot stick, stared at us with a pair of dark, hollow sockets in its face, where eyes should have been.

Cowering in fear, Charlie and I hugged each other tightly, our loud screams rending the air.

WAS THAT AN ALIEN???

'Wh-what is that creature?' Charlie stammered with panic in his voice. 'Wh-why is it looking at us with those creepy, eyeless sockets???'

My heart pounding hard, I watched in terror as the alien-like creature stood frozen several feet away from us, its eyeless sockets trained on Charlie and I.

When the creature suddenly flinched a little, I was startled, and together with Charlie, we retreated a few steps backward, transfixed by the scary-looking creature.

'I hope it doesn't come near us,' Charlie said, his arms wrapped around me.

The creature, which had been standing still like a statue, began to tilt its head sideways, as though it was doing some sort of neck exercise.

'Wh-what do you want?!' I said to the creature, my voice trembling.

'Robin, it's an alien,' Charlie guessed. 'I don't think it understood what you said. It probably wants to … EAT US!' A terrified yelp escaped Charlie's throat, and I could see that his face had become competely ashen.

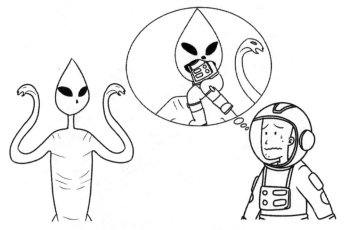

'Charlie, don't say that!' I scolded, my blood turning cold at the thought that we could be eaten alive by the horrid-looking creature.

The creature suddenly moved, putting forward one sinuous leg, which looked like the long, thin body of a snake, its feet shaped like the inflatable hood of a cobra.

Startled, Charlie and I staggered backward and edged away from the creature until our bodies finally touched the wall, restricting further movement.

'We're trapped!' Charlie shrieked, his eyes widening in horror as the creature slowly approached us, its snakey hands undulating ominously in the air.

My eyes darted everywhere, searching for an exit, but there was none! The door, which had appeared behind the creature, had already vanished into thin air, like magic.

With its hands stretched out into the air, as though they were meant to attack us, the strange creature walked sinuously across the room toward us, and when it was about a mere metre away from us, I thought that we were sure going to be GONE for good.

When the creature finally opened its mouth, razor-sharp teeth protruding out from the corners, my stomach clenched hard. 'You HUMANS . . . our SLAVES,' were the wheezy-sounding words that came out from the creature's mouth.

My jaw dropped. Did the creature just talk to us, in simple English? I thought the creature was planning to eat Charlie and I, but apparently, it deemed us as 'slaves'.

'Slaves???' Charlie cried incredulously. 'Me a slave? I'm no one's slave, okay?'

The creature, which didn't have any eyebrows, reacted in anger, the upper outline of its sockets curving into an 'angry' look, and fear shot up through my chest. What would it do to us now that we had provoked it?

'You slave, you slave,' the creature repeated wheezily, then turned around.

The wall, where the door had first appeared, glowed into the outline of a doorway again, where two more creatures, looking like exact duplicates of the first one, strode out, flanked the first creature, and stared at us with their soul-less, hollow sockets.

'There are three of them!' Charlie cried, clinging to me with his trembling arms. 'I think they're all aliens form another planet!'

'And since we're held captive by them,' I said in deep fear, 'I think they want to make us their slaves!'

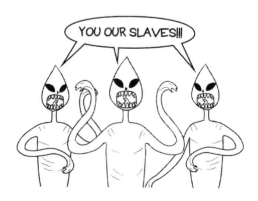

'SLAVES!' the first alien bellowed wheezily, its snakey limbs pointing at Charlie and I

Seconds later, the two other aliens, which had stood beside the first alien like bodyguards, sprang towards us, grabbed both Charlie and I with their creey-looking snakey limbs, and dragged us towards the glowing door.

'NOOOOOOO!!!' Charlie and I wailed our lungs out, our feet screeching against the steely grey floor as the two crazy aliens hauled us away.

I struggled to break free, but the aliens overpowered us with their brute strength.

The aliens thrust us into the other side of the doorway, dragged us down a extremely bright, narrow passageway towards the end of another door, and pushed us through into a dark, shabby chamber with dirty-looking walls; overhead, dozens of iron cages, which were big enough to fit a rooster, hung from the ceiling.

WHAT IN THE WORLD WAS THIS PLACE???

Charlie screeched in horror at the sight of the hanging cages.

'Robin, now I'm REALLY scared!' Charlie said, glancing nervously at me.

The aliens, which still had us in their vice-like grip, suddenly floated up towards the cages like specters, unlatched the doors of the cages, and heaved both Charlie and I into our own separate cages, side by side. They then latched the cages shut, floated downwards, and flanked the first creature, which was looking up at us with some sort of satisfaction on its face, indicated by the twisted upper outline of its eye sockets.

'LET US OUT!!!' I cried desperately, tears in my eyes. I'd never ever see my parents, or my friends again. I'd never ever eat my favourite Sarawak Laksa again. I'd be a mere distant memory, so far from Earth that nobody would be able to find me.

Charlie and I both rattled our cages, which began swinging creakily.

'You no escape,' the first alien said, its limbs constantly undulating eerily. 'You become slave. We bring you back to planet. Our planet. Far from your home. You work for us. You our slave.'

'We don't want to be SLAVES!' Charlie snapped, his cheeks flushed red. 'I'm the son of a VIP on planet Earth, and Robin...' Charlie glanced quickly at me, 'is the son of a billionaire. We ain't no SLAVES, FYI!'

The first alien shook its head disapprovingly, its eye sockets narrowing slightly at us.

'We bring you to our planet now,' the first alien continued, while the two other flanking aliens remained stationary, as though they would only move under the command of the first alien.

'We don't want to go to your planet!' I yelled, the fury rising over my fear.

'You go,' the first alien said. 'You slave. We show you your new life.'

Then, the three aliens whirled around, facing the wall behind them, where the door had already vanished; a glowing screen, which appeared to be about sixty-inch wide, materialized with some fuzzy, static lines across it.

Moments later, the static lines disappeared, followed by moving images on the screen.

When Charlie and I saw what was shown on the screen, our jaws dropped in horror.

On the screen, two boys, which looked like a computer-generated -imagery versions of Charlie and I, were heaving heavy-looking bricks the size of a large hippopotamus, their sweaty faces looking completely miserable.

'OH MY GOD!' Charlie cried incredulously. 'Is-is that a simulation of us working as slaves on planet alien? I can't believe this!'

I gaped at the horrifying scene playing before my eyes on the screen, where Charlie and I were seen doing hard manual labour in a deserted, desolate place against a steely blue-colored cityscape in the distance, looking like we were forced into doing construction work for the aliens.

I couldn't believe how technologically advanced these alien species were. They were able to instantly simulate our new lives as slaves on their alien planet, projecting our actual appearances onto the scene. They were indeed light years ahead of the human world!

'My nails!' Charlie screeched, when he saw that the simulation had gotten too realistic, showing his nails breaking as he lifted a heavy brick.

MY POOR NAILS! ARE THERE GOING TO BE ANY MANICURES ON PLANET ALIEN?

The simulation finally ended, and the same blank steely gray wall reappeared when the screen dissipated out of sight.

'This your new life,' the first alien said, turning to face us. 'When we reach our planet, you become slave. We go back to our planet now.' Then, the first alien turned around, in syncronization with the two other aliens and walked towards the wall, where the glowing door materialized; the three aliens eventually disappeared through the door, which vanished into thin air. Charlie and I were now alone in the godforsaken dark chamber.

'We have to get out of here!' I said urgently, rattling the cage with my hands.

'But how?' Charlie retorted. 'Our cages are locked!'

My eyes darted everywhere around the chamber, looking for a possible way to escape.

There was not a single door in sight; I wondered how the aliens had conjured up the glowing door in a seemingly magical way. So how were we supposed to escape when there was NO door?

'Robin,' Charlie said, tinkering with the padlock on his cage. 'With the alien technology we have just witnessed, you would think the stupid aliens would use something hi-tech to lock us up. They probably think that slaves deserve shabby locks.'

I looked down at my own padlock, which seemed too thick to be easily rent apart. There was no way I could bite through that lock without crushing my teeth.

'We don't have the tools to break the lock, Robin,' Charlie continued dejectedly. 'Face it ... we're doomed! You and I are going to be slaves!'

I fidgeted with the lock, my anxious mind racing with possibilites. Could we pummel the padlock apart with our fists? I looked carefully at the padlock, and my heart sank. Our fists would be completely bruised if we did that.

Charlie, who looked completely hopeless by now, started to belt out a song in an off-pitch voice. 'Baby you're knockin' but there ain't no way I'm ever letting you in . . . not again . . . so keep on knockin', knockin', knockin' . . . '

'Charlie, your singing can cause birds to fall from the sky,' I said drily. 'What's up with you?'

Charlie scoffed, looking like a madman who had gone through enough stress. 'I'm just so depressed and scared, Robin. I miss home. I miss my mom and dad. I miss everything. The thought that we're being shipped off to planet alien now completely petrifies me . . . and makes me feel borderline crazy.'

Charlie continued singing, and I asked him, 'What song is that? I've never heard of it.'

'It's called "Knockin" by Freddie Stroma. Alibaba always plays this song in his car, so I've gotten used to it.' Charlie went back to singing.

The lyrics lingered in my head. 'Baby you're knockin' but there ain't no way I'm ever letting you in ... not again ... so keep on knockin', knockin', knockin' ... '

Knocking?

I suddenly brightened up a little when an epiphany struck me, and I got a little too excited and banged my head against the roof of the tiny, cramped cage when I tried to get to my feet. Well, Charlie and I had to squat inside our cages, which were too small to have a full standing body inside.

'Charlie, I just had a brilliant idea!' I cried, gripping the bars of my cage tightly. 'This may work!'

Charlie stopped singing and looked at me as though I was crazy. 'What may work?'

ROBIN, YOU HAVE A CRAZY LOOK IN YOUR EYES.

I began singing what Charlie had sung: 'Baby you're knockin' but there ain't no way I'm ever letting you in . . . not again . . . so keep on knockin', knockin', knockin' . .'

Charlie rolled his eyes. 'Why are you singing my song?'

With a slight grin, I gripped my cage's bars with both hands firmly, rattled the cage violently, and swung it, with all my might, towards Charlie.

When my cage banged against his, Charlie let out a horrified scream. 'What are you doing, Robin? Have you gone entirely mad???'

'Charlie, do what I'm doing,' I said, still swinging the cage. 'If we both swing our cage and bang it against one another, the padlocks may break apart!'

Charlie widened his eyes. 'You are so right, Robin! It's worth a shot!'

So with both the padlocks on our cages facing each other, Charlie and I begin thrusting our cage forward; our cages clunked hard against each other, causing us to shake violently inside.

After several more attempts, the sound of breaking metal pierced the air, and I watched as pieces of the broken padlocks showered down onto the floor.

The padlocks had been removed! It was now our chance to escape!

'Hurry!' I cried. 'Let's get out now while we can!' I pushed the door of the cage open with both feet, scrambled through the opening, and tumbled down onto the floor with a painful, loud thud. Charlie followed suit.

'Ouch!' Charlie groaned, slowly getting to his feet, rubbing his backside. 'My ass hurts!'

'It will be more than your ass that gets hurt if we don't get out of here!' I warned, darting around the shabby room, my hands feeling the walls for any doors. 'I can't find any doors! How did the aliens conjure up the door? Do they have some kind of magic powers?'

'Robin, we're doomed,' Charlie cried forlornly, after circling the entire room. 'There are no doors. We're still trapped!'

I tugged at my hair, panicking. 'What are we supposed to do? Say "hocus pocus" to get the door to appear?'

'Wait a minute!' Charlie cried, his finger pointing to something towards the far end of the room.

I followed his gaze, and saw a tiny vent at the top of of the wall; it looked narrow, but might be enough to fit one person through at a time. 'That's our escape!' I said triumphantly, feeling hopeful.

'But how do we get up there?' Charlie pointed out. 'It's quite high up the wall. We'd need a ladder.'

Charlie and I dashed toward the small vent, stopped just right below it and looked upwards, sizing it up.

'What if you lean against the wall,' I said, 'and I climb on top of you to get into the vent?'

Charlie shook his head. 'It looks too high to reach even if I gave you a boost.'

I sighed. Charlie was right. From what I could gauge, the vent looked pretty high, at least ten feet.

Then, my eyes roamed the dozens of cages in the room, my mind racing for a way out. Every cage, which hung from the wall by a sturdy-looking shackle, was uneven in height. One cage appeared higher than the other, and one particular cage hung near to the vent.

I began to perk up, an idea forming in my mind. 'Charlie! There's a way to get to that vent. We'll need to parkour across the cages toward the vent!'

Charlie gasped, his eyes twinkling for the very first time. 'Robin, you're a genius! Come on, let's do it before the aliens get here!'

Next second, Charlie and I were rushing toward the lowest-hanging cage, which required Charlie to give me a boost onto the top of the dome-shaped roof of the cage. From the roof of the cage, I stretched both hands out towards Charlie and grabbed him up onto the top of the cage with me.

'Try not to move too much,' I said warningly. 'The cage shakes.'

Charlie nodded, and we began leaping from one cage to another, with me taking the lead.

Several moments later, we finally reached the highest cage, which hung the closest to the vent, just a metre apart.

'Alright, I'm going in first,' I volunteered. With Charlie holding my legs firmly, I began to stretch my whole body, slowly, towards the vent. I grabbed the edge of the vent with both arms, slowly squeezing myself through the narrow gap, and finally pulled both legs in when Charlie released them. I was finally inside the vent!

'Charlie, give me your hands!' I said, my hands outstretched.

Charlie sprang toward me and grabbed my hands, his legs propped against the top of the cage for support; once he had squeezed in halfway into the vent, he let his legs go off from the cage and wriggled all the way in.

'You did it!' I cried ecstatically.

Suddenly, I heard the sound of a mystical twinkle coming from the room below, but I couldn't see what made that sound as Charlie was blocking my view of the vent's entryway.

'What's that sound, Charlie?' I murmured, my breath caught in my throat.

'Oh no!' Charlie whispered urgently. 'I see the same glowing door materializing, and out come the three scary-looking aliens!'

'SLAVIZES GAGA WAZA???' the first alien screamed gibberish in a wheezy voice, sounding completely enraged.

Charlie jerked his head towards me. 'Robin, hurry! Move along now! We need to make a run for it! I think the aliens are going to see me as I'm the closest to the vent's entryway!' Charlie turned around toward the vent. 'Oh no! The aliens have spotted me! One of them is pointing up at me!'

'SLAVIZES!' the same alien voice boomed. 'SIZA LOCO LOLA VENTI SEEBA!'

THEY FOUND US!!!

Charlie and I started scrambling fast along the vent. Fortunately for us, the vent had narrow slits at every corner, which offered some illumination from the rooms below it, so we could see our way.

'I see something at the end of this vent!' I said, my pulse pounding in my ears. 'It looks like a ... vent covering!'

Charlie and I finally reached the end of the vent, where it was sealed with a circular metallic covering. It seemed a little loose, so I gave it a push, and the covering toppled outward and bright lights from the room below streamed in.

I thrust my head forward and looked downward at a brightly lit room, where neat rows of shelves lined the walls, with glass bottles sitting on them. I took a deep gulp when I realized that those glass bottles contained what looked like human skulls!

'SLAVE! SLAVE! SLAVE!' the same wheezy alien sound suddenly boomed, sending goosebumps across my entire body.

Charlie jerked his head around and screamed. 'OH NO! THE ALIENS ARE ON OUR TAILS! THEY'RE BEHIND US!'

Next second, one by one, Charlie and I pushed ourselves out through the vent and toppled down onto the floor, which looked to be about five feet from the vent.

We scrambled to our feet, groaning in slight pain, and holding Charlie's hands firmly, we both scuffled through the room, knocking down row after row of shelves, which crashed down onto the floor with the sound of breaking bottles. Ahead of me, I saw a door with a large metal wheel knob. A door! Finally!

Beside the door was a metal container filled with junks of all sorts, from metal scraps to space helmets. Wait, were those OUR space helmets??? It seemed that the container was used to specifically store 'human' collections.

'Quick!' I said. 'Let's grab our helmets and find a way out!'

Quickly, Charlie and I fixed the helmets onto our heads.

I jerked my head around and saw that the three aliens were now down from the vent and onto the floor, and were scrambling over the toppled shelves; occasionally, they slipped on the occasionally they slipped and fell on the floor which was now littered with the liquid from the broken glass bottles.

'We need to HURRY!' I cried. 'They're gaining on us!'

I frantically turned the wheel knob all the way to its end and tried to push the door open, but it wouldn't budge! We were TRAPPED! 'The door won't open!'

I stole a quick glance around. The aliens were fast gaining on us, just a few metres away!

'NO!!!' Charlie yelled, squeezing me tightly with his hands.

All of a sudden, the door in front of me swung open with a strong creaking noise. Both Charlie and I swiveled our heads from the aliens to the door, and when we saw what stood in the doorway, we gasped in astonishment.

A tall male astronaut, clad in a spacesuit and a space helmet, floated at the doorway, which led outside to space! He looked so familiar that I had to do a double-take at the astronaut's round weary-looking face, which was dotted with moustache around him plum lips.

'DAD???' Charlie cried, his eyes bulging in deep shock. It wasn't Alibaba, Charlie's stepfather, but Anson Kong, Charlie's biological father, who was mysteriously right in front of us in the flesh! I knew that Anson was an astronaut, but why was he here, of all places? How did he end up outside the alien spaceship???

I guess Anson would have some explaining to do later, as the aliens were now hot on our trail.

'Quick, follow me!' Anson barked, and Charlie and I followed him hurriedly out of the door. Anson then slammed the door shut and turned the wheel knob to lock it in place so the aliens couldn't come out. There was a loud thudding on the other side of the door; it seemed the aliens were trying to open it.

'The door cannot be opened if one of the wheel knobs is locked in place,' Anson said. 'That was how you guys were able to get out. I helped you two unlock it from the other side of the door.'

'B-but . . . Dad,' Charlie began, choking back emotions. 'H-how come you're here?'

Anson sighed, his eyes clouding over. 'Believe it or not . . . I was also a prisoner in the aliens' spaceship, but I managed to escape. The padlock of the my cage was a bit shoddy so I managed to break it with my fist when the aliens were not around.' Anson ungloved one hand, showing deep bruises on it.

'You were captured by the aliens???' I said incredulously.

Anson nodded. 'Yes. I got sucked into their spaceship about . . . ' Anson glanced at his silver watch, 'ten hours ago during my solo space expedition. I pray that my crew on-site are now on the search for me and will come rescue us in a matter of time. The aliens wanted to turn me into their SLAVE.'

Charlie cringed. 'Tell me all about it.'

'I actually knew you guys were held captive,' Anson said. 'I was surprised when I found out that it was you two.'

Both Charlie and I gasped. 'HOW?'

'I was the first to escape using the same route you guys did. I went through the vent into the glass-bottle room, and discovered that our space helmets were stored there. In case you didn't notice, there was actually a CCTV screen at the furthest corner, livestreaming different locations of this spaceship. When I saw you TWO, I was reeled with shock, then I realized I had to save you guys. But you two were smart. I saw you breaking the padlocks with pendulum-style momentum, and making your way through the vent. So all I had to do was wait behind this door, and time it right. Once you guys reached there, I quickly opened the door for your escape and shut it back before the aliens had a chance to seize you.'

'Wow, Dad,' Charlie cried, on the verge of tears. 'That's so . . . heroic.' Charlie seemed as though he wanted to give Anson a hug, but Anson appeared defensive, a look of urgency on his face.

'Look, we got to skedaddle out of here now while the aliens are trapped in that room, figuring a way to get out,' Anson said, darting over to a nearby floating white rocket-shaped device, which was about seven-foot long. 'I stole this from the bottle-glass room earlier. The aliens must have gotten their hands on it somehow. It's human-made.' Anson looked at a metre reading strip on its edge. 'It has enough fuel to last us for about a ten-minute trip.'

We scrambled onto the rocket as though we were riding a motorbike, and gripped the handheld bar firmly to prevent from slipping off. Then, Anson activated the rocket with a few presses on the control panel, and the rocket zoomed through space, away from the alien spaceship!

'Wheeeeeeee!!!' we whooped as the rocket sailed ahead.

'Keep a lookout for any nearby space shuttles so we can get immediate help,' Anson said, 'presumably human ones, not alien spacehips.' We couldn't help but laugh, relieved to have escaped.

I didn't catch sight of any human space shuttles, but I thought I saw something familiar. 'Look! I see the Moon!'

Anson steered the rocket towards the Moon, parked right at its edge and we hopped out onto the Moon, just as the rocket ran out of fuel.

'I guess we're stuck on the Moon,' Charlie grumbled slightly. 'I guess it's better than being locked up in the alien spaceship!'

Before I could form a reply, a beeping sound rent the air. I looked down at the oxygen reading level on my sleeve, which was flashing an ominous red. 'My oxygen level is running low!'

'SO IS MINE!' both Charlie and Anson cried.

My heart started thumping and I began to have difficulty breathing from the slowly draining oxygen—an imminent death sentence.

'Robin!!!' Charlie said anxiously, holding me in a tight hug. 'I so don't want to die! You know that, right?'

'I know!' I shrieked, my whole body trembling. 'I don't want to die either. But what choice do we have?'

As we lamented on our imminent death, a sudden boom pierced the air, sounding like a thunder rumple, and immediately, we jerked our heads upwards to the source of the noise, our eyes bulging in sheer astonishment; a fiery, long-tailed object thundered past above us, as though it was a huge kite on fire.

'It's the darkensom meteor!!!' I cried, my eyes riveted on the strange meteor, which bathed the moon in luminous orange light.

'The darken-what???' Charlie said, a flabbergasted look on his sunken face.

As I sat there, completely transfixed by the unexpected emergence of the meteor, a ray of hope began to fill me. 'Wait a minute!' I said, suddenly feeling slightly hopeful. 'Do you remember what Spacey said about the darkensom meteor?'

'NO!' Charlie barked. 'Do I look like some kind of a space nerd? That's Ken's alley ... if only he were here with us!!!'

'I know what the darkensom meteor is, so let me explain,' Anson offered. 'When a meteor, which is a rock, enters Earth's atmosphere, it burns up, due to friction with air. So when it lights up in space, it means that there are pockets of AIR nearby!!!!!'

Charlie's eyes widened. 'AIR???'

I clutched Charlie's hand firmly, eyes welling with joyful tears. 'Yes! Do you know what this means? It means that there is OXYGEN nearby, so what we need to do now is to locate the air pockets!'

'But how? I thought they were invisible!'

'We'll have to follow the trail of the darkensom meteor to where the oxygen is!' Anson said urgently, starting to make a move. 'Hurry! We don't have much time left!'

With the three of us holding one another's hand in solidarity, Charlie, Anson and I scrambled our way towards the Moon's edge, and hovered about at the spot where we thought we had last seen the darkensom meteor disappear.

As we began combing around for the darkensom meteor, I felt a tight sensation in my chest, struggling for air. I could see that both Charlie and Anson were having difficulty with their breathing too.

'Hurry!' I blustered, panic rising within me. 'The pocket of air must be nearby!'

When another sharp beep pinged, my eyes swiveled to the reading metre on my sleeve, which read: 0 % OXYGEN LEVEL!

There was NO MORE oxygen left, and by then, I couldn't breathe anymore, my lungs feeling as though they were pressed under a ton of bricks. Petrified and extremely agitated, I flailed about uncontrollably and violently, the lack of oxygen in my brain causing me to hallucinate, then with the rise of delirius panic, I impetuously, without meaning to, removed my space helmet and flung it away; Charlie and Anson, in the same state of wild delirium as I, did the same.

'I C-C-CAN'T BREATHE!!!' Charlie croaked miserably, his hands gripping his throat firmly.

Where was that pocket of air? I wondered desperately, choking for air, my chest heaving up and down fast. I felt weaker and weaker by the minute, life gradually ebbing away from my body. Where was that airibum???

As both Charlie and Anson were struggling for air, they flailed about wildly, thrust themselves around haphazardly, and by accident, bumped hard against me, pushing me a couple of feet away from the Moon's edge.

Suddenly, I felt a strange, airy sensation surging through my body, as though I was a helium balloon being pumped with air. Seconds later, I could feel air rushing back into my lungs like a soothing balm, and I was gradually able to mentally focus again, my delusional, pain-racked brain slowly beginning to recover.

Most importantly, I felt as though I could breathe again!

I must be have stumbled upon the pocket of air—airibum—by accident, and I could feel strength gradually returning to my weakened body. I jerked my head sideways and watched in horror as Charlie and Anson were both losing consciousness, eyes closed on their blanched faces. In a split second, I darted towards them, held both tight in my arms and dragged them towards the airibum.

'Come on, you guys!' I cried, my stomach deeply clenched, holding and shaking their seemingly lifeless bodies in my arms.

They still didn't move, and I thought that they were really gone.

'No!!!' I wailed, my body convulsing uncontrollably. But when I looked down, I began to realize that it wasn't my body shaking. It was Charlie's!

Charlie's body, which was limp and lifeless, had started to tremble wildly, his arms and legs flailing about and his eyes blinking rapidly, as though he was possessed by a demon. It dawned on me that he probably reacted that way due to the sudden rush of oxygen entering his lungs. Moments later, his body calmed down considerably, and he jerked a glance at me, color returning to his face.

'I can BREATHE!' Charlie cried deliriously, a weak smile plastered on face. 'Wh-what happened???'

Seconds later, Anson also regained consciousness, his bleary eyes blinking. 'Wow . . . we were almost . . . ' He gulped. 'GONE.'

'We're now floating in the spot where the airibum is!' I said, throwing my arms around Charlie in a tight hug, so relieved that Charlie and I were now alive thanks to this miraculous, small pocket of air floating around in space.

Charlie arched an eyebrow. 'Airi-what-bum? Airi has a bum?'

I shook my head, laughing. 'No, silly! Have you forgotten about what Spacey said about strange pockets of air floating around in space?' Seeing the confused look on Charlie's face, I began to explain to Charlie about what an airibum was.

'I'm so glad we stumbled upon this airbus,' Charlie said gratefully. 'We could have died!!!'

'Airibum, not airbus,' I corrected with a wry smile. 'Yes, I know … it was a serendipitous encounter with the airibum, I suppose.' Suddenly, the ray of hope, which had come upon me briefly, was completely dashed by a sinking feeling in the pit of my stomach.

Charlie noticed the change in my mood. 'What's wrong, Robin? Why are you so glum all of a sudden? Shouldn't we be celebrating our great survival due to this weird oxygen pocket in space called the … um … airi-airi-bum? Yay, I got it right, I think.'

I sighed. 'Charlie, we're literally lost in space! We can have all the airibums in space, but if no one ever finds us … what's the point? We cannot survive alone on oxygen, and on top of that, we need food and water.

I can't imagine being stuck here forever!' I said tearily, curling my body in a miserable foetal position, the hopeless sense of desolation washing over me.

We were never going to be found, and we were sure to perish in space. Hope had completely abandoned us.

'Wait a minute!' Anson cried suddenly, startling both Charlie and I 'W-w-what's that thing hovering along the Moon's edge?'

Instantly, I swiveled my eyes towards the 'thing' Anson had mentioned, squinted my eyes for a better look, then when I saw what it was, my eyes widened in recognition.

'It's the CAMERA DRONE!' I shrieked, feeling suddenly hopeful again. 'Remember that drone that was used to live-broadcast my birthday celebration on the Moon to the entire world? Someone must have forgotten to bring it back to our space shuttle!'

Charlie jaw dropped. 'Of course I remember! Who else in this universe has their birthday on the Moon broadcast for the entire world to see?' Then, he gasped, his eyes twinkling. 'Oh my God! I just had an epiphany. Are you thinking what I'm thinking???'

'Of course! We're the best of friends, with an absolutely great mental connection!' I winked at Charlie, and he laughed, giving me a high-give.

Next moment, Charlie and I floated towards the floating camera drone and positioned ourselves right in front of the high-definition camera, preparing to send our SOS to the world, as Anson watched quietly from behind, with a slight glee on his face.

'Hello, EARTHLINGS!' Charlie shrilled, his hands waving wildly at the camera.

I rolled my eyes. 'Earthlings? You make us sound like aliens from another planet.'

'If you can hear us,' Charlie continued, his eyes filled with desperation, 'we're sending you an SOS from space! We're stuck on the Moon here, and we're in DIRE need of help!'

'Yes, we need help, PRONTO!' I cried, waving my hands in front of the camera. 'I hope you see our video message and send a rescue team immediately, because WE'RE LOST IN SPACE!'

MOMENTS LATER . . .

'Did I look good on camera?' Charlie asked haughtily, moments after Charlie and I had been successfully rescued by the space rescue team, who was urgently dispatched to the Moon as a result of our SOS video going viral.

I sighed. 'Charlie, is this your most prominent concern of the century? Looking good on camera? We could have died in space, and no one would have ever know!' Just saying those last words sent shivers down my spine.

'Hello, but did you know the drone camera is HD?' Charlie went on shamelessly. 'I have a zit on my left cheek, and what if the whole world saw it in HD?' Charlie said with a look of horror, fingering a barely visible pimple on his left cheek. 'I just hope that I didn't look like an alien with a zit.'

I shook my head, chuckling in spite of myself, at Charlie's dramatic flair. There were times I wanted to strangle Charlie for being borderline annoying, but it was his eccentricity that created sparks in our friendship; life is NEVER boring with Charlie around.

I was so glad with how everything had turned out. Right after Charlie and I had recorded our SOS video, which had, by now, been seen by millions in the world, the space authorities saw the video and immediately sent out a rescue team to the Moon. I couldn't help but thank God for all the small things, which led to our rescue.

If it wasn't for the airibum, we'd have been dead.

If it wasn't for the camera drone, NO ONE would have ever found out.

When the space rescue team arrived in a small, cream-colored space shuttle half the size of a commercial aeroplane, three astronauts, two males and one female, had rushed out, zoomed towards Charlie, Anson and I, and ensured that we were okay; they had refilled our oxygen supply via a portable oxygen machine, and had even given us some space food, which was pre-packed, in case we were hungry.

Charlie, Anson and I were then ushered comfortably into the rescue space shuttle, where we were seated on a long bench facing the entryway.

'Where are we headed now?' Charlie asked, buckling up.

'We're flying you two back to Earth,' the muscular male astronaut, who had a tattoo on his neck, said.

'But what about our parents?' I cried, the faces of Mom and Dad, and our my friends, popping into my head. 'Our friends? Are they still in space? Or headed back to Earth already?'

I SO CAN'T WAIT TO HEAD BACK TO PLANET EARTH.

The muscular male astronaut smiled quietly, as though he was hiding a secret.

'ROBIN! CHARLIE!' Familiar voices boomed.

'Oh my God! I thought we would never see you again!'

'I was so dead worried when I discovered that you two were gone!'

One by one, familiar faces popped through the entryway, and I gasped, competely stunned. They were my family and friends! How on earth—I mean space—did this happen?

Mom and Dad, who were the first to reach me, gave me a tight hug, as though they were never ever letting go. Soon, Manda, Alibaba, Ken, Siti, Chloe and Devi bunched up around Charlie and I, squeezing both of us in a wonderful sweet embrace.

'We're so glad you TWO are okay!'

When they saw Anson huddled at the corner, their faces plastered with confusion. Manda, among everyone, looked like she had seen a ghost, her eyes almost protruding out.

'What is my ex-husband doing here???' Manda cried in disbelief. 'Anson Kong! I can't believe you're here!'

So I began to explain to everyone how Anson had come into the picture, how he had been captured by the aliens—just like Charlie and I—and how he had escaped and eventually rescued us.

What a small world, wasn't it? To have met Charlie's biological father in space ... when Charlie and I had been talking so much about Anson during our Moon rendezvous, and then he had just appeared in our lives once again. The universe, really, worked in mysterious ways.

Charlie's father is an astronaut, so it was no wonder we chanced upon him in space, albeit in 'weird' circumstances.

Manda was so grateful when she heard the rescue story that she wrapped her ex-husband in a hug, much to Alibaba's slight disappointment, who seemed to go a little green with envy.

When the huggy reunion had gotten less intense, I asked, 'How-how are you guys here?'

'Simple,' Dad said with a smile. 'We have been in constant communication with the rescue team. They gave us their coordinates, so we followed them all the way here to you guys!'

'You mean Shuttle Robin is right here?' I asked, widening my eyes.

'Yup, it's parked just right behind the rescue space shuttle, and if you want, you can follow us back home.'

I jerked my head towards the muscular male astronaut, who was watching the entire family reunion. 'C-can we go over to our own space shuttle?'

The astronaut smiled. 'Sure, I don't see why not. It seems that both you, Charlie and Anson are in good condition, so there's no need to keep you here any longer for observation.'

I pumped my fist into the air, overjoyed that I'd soon be rejoining my family and friends once more in the safety of Shuttle Robin.

Meanwhile, Alibaba and Manda wrapped their arms so tightly around Charlie that it seemed to nearly suffocate him to death.

'Charlie,' Manda choked up, eyes welling up. 'I had been worried sick about you, and because of that, I think I've grown extra wrinkles around my left eye. I probably need more Botox when we return to Earth.'

Charlie flinched a little, a wry look on his face. 'Mom, not your wrinkles, Botox and whatnot again. You care more about your face than my well-being?'

Manda's jaw dropped in astonishment, as though Charlie had said a curse word. 'No, no, Charlie! You mean the absolute world to me! How could I choose Botox over my only son? You are more important than all the Botox in the world!'

Charlie's lips curved into an earnest smile. 'Oh, mom. I love you.'

'I love you too!' Manda said, and the mother and son went for another round of hugs.

'Me too!' Alibaba said passionately, joining the family group hug.

As if Charlie's family reunion wasn't melodramatic enough, my parents had to get richly emotional in a scene fit for Hallmark Channel.

'Did you know that my heart almost shattered to a gazillion pieces when we found out that you were missing?' Mom choked, almost in tears.

'Oh, my precious Robin,' Dad said, also looking like he was on the verge of tears. 'When you guys went missing, I thought we were never going to see you again. But thank God you guys did that SOS video, or we'd never have found you!'

Why was everyone around me crying as though they were attending my funeral? I was alive, for God's sake. Seeing everyone in tears made me want to cry along.

'I guess everything happens for a reason,' I said, getting teary-eyed, recalling the moment when Charlie and I were stuck on the Moon, where we bonded much deeper than ever before, showed our vulnerable side, and learned to be grateful for every breath that we breathed, not taking things for granted in life. Sometimes, it takes darkness to show us the light.

Dad gave me a mock stern, warning look. 'Don't you ever disappear on us like that ever again. We had the greatest scare of a lifetime, you know,' Dad paused briefly, his eyes softening, as Mom huddled beside him, 'We love you, Robin.'

'I love both of you, Mom and Dad,' I said, as we tangled ourselves in a warm family embrace.

'Can the hugging fest stop already?' Charlie grumbled good-naturedly, and we all laughed. 'I'm feeling so warm and cuddly that my insides are starting to light up with fire.'

Then, Charlie turned to look at Anson, who had been watching the reunion from a corner, an unreadable expression on his face.

'Hey . . . um . . . Dad,' Charlie said awkwardly, 'would you like to join us back home in our space shuttle?'

Anson smiled. 'It's alright, Charlie. My own crew is coming to get me soon. I'm following them back home.'

'Okay. Will I be seeing you around again . . . um . . . soon?'

Anson winked. 'You betcha.'

As I watched my family and friends huddled close around me, I couldn't help but feel a beautiful sense of warmth surging inside me.

Space was one desolate, cold, dark infinity, but it can instantly feel like home when the people you love surround you. Home is where your family and friends are.

A WEEK LATER

'OH MY GOD! My zit is so crystal clear!'

I heaved a huge sigh, shaking my head at Charlie's absurdity; he was haranguing about his zit for the hundredth time.

My friends and I were gathered at my mansion's spacious den on a beautiful Sunday morning, where the warm rays of the sun filtered through the silky cream curtains. I had invited everyone over for a special televised viewing of the recent rescue mission in space, on my cinema-worthy, giant one-hundred-inch LED television, which showed footages of how the space crew came to rescue Charlie and I

Everyone was especially transfixed by the main footage, which showed Charlie and I talking in front of the camera drone, sending an SOS message.

By now, everyone in the world had seen the infamous footage, as every major news outlet had shown it.

For the past week, news reporters had been flocking to our houses, bombarding us with questions, and of course, Charlie, being the attention seeker that he was, LOVED every minute of it. Charlie thought that he'd achieved some kind of celebrity status.

'I probably should hire a personal fashion stylist,' Charlie had said haughtily. 'I mean, I'm going to be on the cover of every major magazine in the world!'

'You mean we,' I had retorted. Seriously, Charlie kept thinking that he was the only one rescued in space. Hello, I was there too. Sometimes, I just wanted to knock some sense into him.

So during the televised viewing in my mansion, where we snacked on popcorn with our eyes glued on the TV, Charlie couldn't stop talking out about his zit, which was shown close-up in high-definition during one of his scenes.

'Nobody's going to remember your zit, okay?' I said to Charlie, savagely crunching the popcorns.

'THE WORLD WILL!' Charlie countered. 'Did you know our SOS footage has been seen in more than fifty countries around the world with ten billion views?! My zit will be remembered forever!' Charlie ended his sentence with a terrified shriek.

Even though I was richly annoyed with Charlie, I couldn't help but chuckle amusedly at his melodrama. Charlie and I might have slightly different personalities and butt heads from time to time, but we would always be the best of friends.

Manda, who was also present at the viewing, offered her two cents to Charlie, 'Charlie, it's a good thing that your zit is being shown worldwide. Who knows that you may secure a deal with a famous beauty brand and become an ambassador for their acne-fighting products?'

Charlie's eyes suddenly sparkled. 'Okay, maybe it's not a totally bad thing if I become world famous. Let's make a toast to my zit.'

Everyone laughed good-naturedly at Charlie's remark, raised glasses to make a toast and jokingly congratulated Charlie on his zit.

When the viewing was over, everybody stayed back a little longer at the den, chatting and sharing funny anecdotes.

Siti, who had obviously gotten a little bored with extended periods of chatting, suggested that we go for a swim at my backyard; my friends were keen on the idea, so we darted through the den's glass sliding doors and out into the backyard, where a humongous guitar-shaped swimming pool sat.

Why was the pool shaped like a guitar? Well, Dad, who used to be a pro guitarist in his high school band, had the pool designed in the shape of a guitar. But now, being the busy man he was, he only had time to play his guitar once in a blue moon.

When everyone changed into their bathing suits, Chloe and Devi jumped headfirst into the pool, causing a tsunami of water to splash onto the pool deck.

'Come join us!' Devi beckoned everyone, flipping her damp hair. 'The water's fine!'

'Sure, right after I'm done with my selfie,' Siti said with a giggle, taking a couple of selfies on the pool deck and flipping her silky hair around like a shampoo model.

One by one, the rest of my friends jumped into the pool, until Charlie and I were the only ones left standing on the pool deck.

'We'll join you guys in a bit,' Charlie cried to the pool crowd, plopping down onto the chaise lounger.

'If you say so,' Ken said sportily, and proceeded to do his usual laps. Did I tell you that Ken was obsessed with swimming? He was the star swimmer of our school, and had clinched almost every medal in swimming competitions.

I swiveled a glance at Charlie, whose eyes seemed to cloud over, as though he had something weighing heavily on his mind.

'What's wrong, Charlie?' I asked, flopping down onto the chaise lounger beside his. 'You look kind of gloomy.'

Charlie sighed. 'I miss him already, you know.'

'Miss who?' I said in mock pretense, even though I clearly knew 'who' he was talking about.

Charlie frowned at me. 'Robin!'

'Okay, okay,' I said, throwing my hands up in surrender. 'But you have your father's number, right? Have you guys been in touch?'

'No,' Charlie said forlornly. 'Initially, we were corresponding, but these past few days, he completely stopped replying to my messages. I even tried calling him, but there's no answer. Do you think he ... ghosted me?'

'Charlie, your father did not GHOST you,' I reassured him. 'Maybe he's too busy at work. He'll eventually reply.'

Charlie sighed, more miserable frown lines deepening his forehead. 'I hope you're right. Or maybe he got into a tragic accident and—'

'Charlie, stop!' I said firmly, giving him a stern look. 'Your father is okay. Give it a few more days, and who knows, he'll reply!'

'Why a few days when it can be NOW?' a husky voice behind us said.

Charlie and I instantly jerked our heads around, our jaws dropping when we saw WHO it was!

Right in the flesh, in front of our very eyes, was none other than Anson Kong, Charlie's biological father, who was dressed in a casual floral print shirt and baby blue Bermuda shorts.

'DAD!' Charlie cried in disbelief, goggling at his father as though he was a mirage in the desert. Charlie immediately got to his feet, sprang over a low bush lining the pool deck, rushed towards his father and wrapped his arms around him.

'Oh, Dad,' Charlie said, tears of joy welling at the corner of his eyes, 'how come you never told me you were coming? You almost gave me a heart attack!'

Anson chuckled. 'Charlie, I wanted it to be a surprise. Your mom knew about this, and I wanted her to keep my surprise visit a secret from you.'

I saw Charlie flick a glance at the den's doorway, where Manda and Alibaba stood watching, hand in hand. Manda had a ecstatic look on her face, but Alibaba didn't look too happy. Did I just sense envy? Alibaba didn't seem excited at all, and maybe it was because he thought that Anson, who had suddenly appeared in Charlie's life, was going to take over his place as Charlie's 'father'.

I guess that only time would tell if Alibaba would warmly accept Anson into the fold, or try to tear Charlie and his biological father apart from each other. Whatever happened in the future between Alibaba and Anson, I'd get my popcorn ready; it would be drama-worthy.

But I'd save my concerns for later, as for now, Charlie seemed really happy to be hanging out with Anson.

'Dad, I want to know you better. For starters, do you like swimming?' Charlie asked, his eyes glancing towards the pool, where the kids were splashing themselves silly.

'Um … yes … but I didn't bring my swim trunks,' Anson said sheepishly.

'Oh, Dad, don't be so serious. Come!' Charlie grabbed one of Anson's hands, then grabbed mine.

WAS CHARLIE CRAZY? What was he thinking?

Then, the three of us, hand in hand, with Charlie in the centre dragging us, scampered towards the pool and jumped into it, with our clothes on.

Anson's head emerged out of the pool, completely soaked. 'Oh my God! I've never done this before in my entire life!' Then, he gave a hearty laugh. 'But it feels good. It really does.'

Charlie and I laughed, playfully splashing more water at Anson, who retaliated by splashing back.

'You can't take life too seriously, Dad,' Charlie said, smiling earnestly. 'Sometimes, you just have to let go and have fun.'

As I watched Charlie and Anson grabbing each other in horseplay and splashing at each other, I smiled widely, swimming further away from the two to give them some father-son time. The bright afternoon shone on them, bringing out their sunny smiles. It was going to be the start of a beautiful relationship.